Paper and Ink

An Anthology

Edited by
Rhoda Greaves, Zoe Southall and L.M. Thompson

Published by **Imprimata**
for and on behalf of The School of English, Birmingham City University.

First published 2013
Compilation © The School of English,
Birmingham City University 2013
Contributions © individual copyright holders

A CIP Catalogue record for this book is available
from the British library

ISBN 978-1-906192-72-3

Designed and typeset in Chaparral Pro (InDCS6)
by Mark Bracey @ Imprimata

Printed in Great Britain

Imprimata

An imprint of InXmedia Limited
www.imprimata.co.uk

Contents

Helen Cross

Helen Cross is the author of three novels, most recently, *Spilt Milk, Black Coffee* (Bloomsbury). She also writes for radio, stage and screen. More at www.helencross.net. Helen is a Fellow of the Institute of Creative and Critical Writing at Birmingham City University, and teaches Fiction on the MA in Writing.

Foreword

Welcome to the 2013 Birmingham City University creative writing anthology. As a reader of this anthology you play an important part in the development of these new voices. For many of those assembled here, you are amongst the first strangers ever to read their work.

These writers, all of them students and staff, are the real deal. By this I mean that they are experienced enough to have long ago stopped believing that they are writing because it is great fun. Or because it feels good. Or because it might make them rich, desired and admired. Or because they believe publishing a book or staging a play is a viable exit strategy from a marriage or teaching.

No, they have all got this far by admitting that writing is a difficult, frustrating, seemingly futile and frequently unpleasant activity. The only reason they keep going is because they've discovered that if they don't they're sad.

This publication is crucial, because every serious writer eventually admits they were lying when they said they were scribbling just for themselves. They were only half honest when they later admitted it was better to share work with a close circle of supporters (with a few enemies thrown in). The truth is that like attention-seeking, personality-disordered addicts we're not just sad if we don't do it, we're as sad if we don't get to share what we've done with lots of strangers.

For some of the writers assembled here this will be their first publication. For less fortunate – or fortunate depending on your experience – others, it will be their last.

Some will too quickly succumb to the comforting control of

self-e-publishing, prematurely uploading and never being heard of again. For others this soft, soon to be obsolete, oblong you hold in your hands could still be a portal to a rewarding, and, yes, possibly, for a very lucky few, a lucrative, life-long, international career.

Whatever happens next, right now, these writers are doing all this work for you, unknown, uncaring, invisible readers. You, who might scan half the book, then go online, under an assumed name, and excitedly ridicule the poems, wittily destroy the stories, and cleverly expose how hilariously talentless are all the authors.

And it's for you, who isn't bitter like the reader above, and would never be deliberately cruel to a new writer, but who has a busy life and many fancier books flirting for your attention. You've also got wonderfully imaginative, creative, story-telling children, and so have many more lovely things to do than read this selection of unknowns. You might not have even paid for the book, or be related to, or sleeping with, anyone in it, so have no incentive whatsoever to even open the cover.

Yet in the most astonishing, stupid, endlessly repeated act of dumb generosity, every writer here is trying to write for you a life-changingly memorable, affecting and moving piece of creative work. Even though they know you don't want it.

The only way to do this, despite all the busy chat about new technologies and the transformation of the writer's life, is the old-fashioned way: the hard way. It takes a long time. It's often grubby and grim. It requires you scratch around in the dirt.

The writers in this anthology have bravely, probably agonisingly, found a voice and confessed their truths; their shames and lies, fears and longings, sins and secrets and are offering these up to you – perhaps in a cunning disguise, such as a rom-com or a flower poem.   And from this act they are hoping to feed themselves and what's left of their family. For the rest of their lives. So, yes, you're allowed to laugh at us – just not anonymously online.

They're not even geniuses, because the writer as genius is, sadly, just a popular myth. There is of course much talent evident here, but, though I hate to say it, talent's not uncommon and good plots are two a penny and few manage to cook a good book from an incredible true-life tale. Most decent works of literary art come down to bloody determination, resilience and carefully learned craft.

As you read you might consider the combination of skills these writers have developed and are displaying. There is the basic, and yet underrated, understanding of grammar: punctuation, tense, rhythm and syntax. Then there is the struggle with point of view, and particularly dialogue, the tussle with not what people say, but through an understanding of the subtle art of subtext, why people say what they say.

Being a natural born liar helps. The storywriters and dramatists are trying to make you believe, and care for, a bunch of imaginary people. If the writer has carefully drawn these lovers and liars with the insight and compassion of an original, humane voice, then, strangely, you may find these creations more memorable and compelling than the real people you know.

That is the greatest hope of these writers. Above all they long to deeply touch, through these memories, images, symbols and made-up people in made-up places doing made up things, just one of you invisible strangers.

To do this they must leap the highest hurdle: structure. From fiction to non-fiction, poetry to drama much comes down to creating the appropriate impact by wrestling with what goes where. The final cut that you see on the following pages is the product of much forehead clutching, desk thumping, furious deleting, desperate resurrecting, self loathing, confusion, insight and euphoria – until the sighing and screaming gives way to resolved cutting and pasting.

Eventually the worst is over, and now you've kindly paid your money and intend to read the story, the connection with you,

Ms Invisible, puts these writers in thrilling and frightening new territory. It certainly takes a certain kind of wild courage to attempt to traditionally publish these days. These hardy writers are trying to board the swanky publishing liner as it's tossed on a rough sea and heading for an iceberg.

It's never been easier to publish a book, and never harder to sell one: never easier to call yourself a writer, and never harder to make a living from that calling. The risk of self-delusion has never been greater.

To make it these writers will need not only the traditional advantages of an elephantine hide, a donkey's frame, and a duck's back to let the cold rain of criticism flow off. In 2013 they'll also need to peacock themselves around a celebrity-saturated new, as well as old, media. No matter how ugly they look, or miserable and anti-social they feel, they'll be expected to ping off artfully windswept photos of themselves and squander their dark talents on cheerful blogs.

So, I trust you will appreciate the hopefulness, courage, energy, determination and learned craft that, against all logic and common sense, has gone into this anthology.

Even more I hope that you will have the pleasure of looking out for, and finding, some of these fantasists still at it, and in something approaching acceptable physical and mental health, in the years to come.

Helen Cross
April 2013

Paper and Ink

Ben Harris

Ben Harris is a fiction writer from Birmingham, England. A writer since the age of four, Ben remains mystified by the correct use of commas and has been known to workshop new material with local ducks. He lives opposite a mortuary in Staffordshire with his pet spider Geoff.

Season's End

Kelly opened her eyes and stared at the light. A plastic bottle of peroxide solution getting dimmer by the moment, maybe another hour of glow left in it.

Roland's grip flexed around her hipbone as he tried to grab hold of a dream and then released with a shiver that set their hammock swinging.

He never complained but she knew he hadn't slept well in weeks. He let out a huff of breath and Kelly watched the cloud of moisture drift down towards the floor as it froze.

The space had been an industrial container before the winter; now it was a few chunks of rust marbled into the walls of an icy cave.

Kelly was reminded of the dream.

She remembered trees though she had never seen a real one up close. The gnarled bark twisting around knots and branches, grass growing through dry dirt under her bare feet. Those old enough to remember said the sun always shone and the air was so warm the snow came down already melted. She remembered her mother telling her how little kids used to run around trying to catch the water with open mouths, drinking from the sky when all the world was a garden.

It was no good dreaming. It was just a world from stories. Somewhere below the ice, the trees still stood but the sun would never reach their bones again.

She turned over in the sleeping bag, Roland's callused hand rough against her waist as she moved. She didn't want to wake him yet. This was the closest thing she got to time alone out here.

Miles and miles today. She hadn't wanted a life spent step-to-step in the frozen wastes, but plans were for fools. It put coin in her hands and food in her belly. More than most got.

She felt the uncomfortable lump of plastic under her and fished it out. The sat-nav was ten years older than she was, and never designed to endure life in the open. Keeping it next to her skin was the only way to stop the liquid crystal screen from freezing up, or the battery dying in minutes instead of days. She didn't turn it on; the jaunty personalised jingle would wake her partner. She knew it was a little more than ten miles as the crows flew, though the thing still wanted them to follow roads buried thirty feet beneath their feet. The relics of the old world didn't know their time was over.

She looked at Roland. Twenty-two years old, though the plains had carved a few lines into his face already. Black hair beginning to grey above his ears as if the frost never had time to melt from him. Half a breath hissed through his clenched teeth before he opened his eyes.

'Morning sleepy.'

She shifted close to him, ignoring the early morning bulge between them. Seventeen was old enough to know that there were parts of a man that woke up before the brain. It wasn't something either of them talked about.

'So what's the plan Roll?'

'We should be moving before it gets light.'

The harsh routine of walk and sleep came easily to him. Kelly had spent less than two years out in the plains. Roland had barely set foot in a town since he was six. She'd slept in the sled as he pulled them through clear nights under black skies on the way here.

He turned over, unzipped their bed and sat up. Cold air rushed into the space he left as he slid on his boots and thumped to the floor. In some ways he was more like the animals here than the people. You never saw a polar bear snoozing when the smell of meat was in the air.

But he wasn't back to his old self yet. In some ways he was still only pretending to be the man that took her on to learn salvaging almost a year ago.

'Slow down Roll, I'll get the tea on.'

She checked the watch her dad gave her. It said it was good for up to two-hundred-metres, though she didn't see how anyone could still read the dials from that far away.

'It's only four,' she said to the rolled up snowsuit under her head, then turned on her front to absorb Roland's fading body heat. She imagined her skin as a sponge leeching as much warmth as she could. Heat was the only vice going some mornings.

'Oh,' he mumbled, distracted. One hand shook the peroxide bottle to get a little more light from the depleted solution, the other flexed on the pommel of the knife at his belt.

She'd never known him as a full-blown junkie but the last two months had come close. One stupid night and he'd gone from two years without KV to just a single morning. At day sixty-three he didn't have nightmares while he was awake anymore but it would be another few months before the residual contaminants dissolved in his muscles. She knew it hurt him more to lie still than to get up but she wished he could've stayed out for a couple more hours. They both needed the rest.

'Here,' she dug around inside her clothes for the tin, opened it and took out the joint. 'I rolled it last night.' Another drug wasn't necessarily the best idea for a recovering addict, but it was the only painkiller they had.

She held the smoke in her lips while her hands fumbled to find her pockets inside the sleeping bag.

'You're a saint Kel.' She could smell nicotine on his rough fingertips as he took it from her mouth and lit it with the Zippo she'd given him. They'd found a whole box of the things in some old key-cutting place under the ice and sold them for food a day later. She'd kept one for him though. It had a picture of a girl in a dress on the front, the wind blowing her hair out behind her as she lit a smoke. To her knowledge he'd never put it down since.

He leaned against the hammock as she wriggled into her cold boots. It wasn't until his third pull that she heard his first relaxed breath of the morning.

'Bad dreams?' she asked him. He was staring into space again. She wouldn't wish KV withdrawal on anyone.

'Yeah.' He didn't elaborate. He didn't talk about it much and when he did there weren't good words to explain the sensation. Only suckers and suicides took the stuff. She had asked him why he'd ever put a vial to his lips in the first place. He said he couldn't remember that far back.

Kelly shut her eyes and counted in her head. On five she would pull back the covers and get out of bed. She got to four and nine tenths before she managed it today.

'Right,' she said as her heels hit the floor. 'Tea first, I think.'

* * *

It was bad today. Ten miles trudging into a steady headwind that forced them both to lean into the sleet to stay upright.

Roland stamped into the snow and managed to get back to the surface. One careless step and he would be up to his thighs in sticky powder. He looked back along the rope to the sled wallowing on its belly, with both skids dragging through the snow. The blizzard had a spiteful edge to it this morning.

If the weather didn't let up before midday they would need to make camp again that night. The surface of the snow was too soft to support his or the sled's weight and that made every step an ordeal. Sometimes he envied Kelly her slight build. In her snowshoes she skipped across the surface like a pixie.

She got a dozen paces ahead before letting him catch up. Kelly held up her hands in a 'T' and then shrugged questioningly. She didn't look tired and Roland knew there was precious little time to stop today.

He pointed a thumb down and Kelly waited for him to reach her.

'Keep going girl, stop fretting over me!'

He shouted to get his meaning through the wind and the insulation protecting her ears. She shrugged and turned back into the sleet. After a few seconds she was well ahead again: she turned and walked backwards a few steps to watch him.

And vanished.

Roland's heart squeezed as he heard her shriek. The safety line connecting them snapped tight and brought him to his knees. Perhaps once he could have dug his toes in and held on but her falling weight yanked him off his feet.

With the wind, he hadn't noticed the slight downwards slope until he was sliding. He dug a deep furrow in the powder as he fought for grip. A semi-conscious thought put his knife in his hand. He slammed it into the ground, but it was like stabbing smoke.

Always a catch… he thought as he tried again and got no grip.

His mind had been on other things. It took him a second or two to make sense of the situation. It only took one more to reach the edge of the crevasse Kelly had tumbled into.

One last stab finally caught something solid. He swung around the knife handle, his shoulder wrenching with a crunch.

Roland remembered the sled behind him just before the left skid hit him in the face.

It went over him and cleared the metre-wide gap in the ice, before the towline jerked and stopped its momentum.

Roland managed to get his other hand on the knife handle and hung on for a heartbeat. Reflex kept his fists clenched tight around the handle and blade both. It cut through his glove and drew a little blood before Roland came to his senses, such as they were.

Hot pain seeped into his skull along with his shoulder and fingers. For a stupid second he regretted getting out of bed that morning. Wished he'd just stayed there for a bit, enjoying the warmth and the soft sounds of his partner breathing.

But he'd made peace with physical discomfort a long time ago. He hung on to the knife with his uninjured hand and snatched at his belt with the other.

The sled rope twanged as he unclipped it from his waist. The salvage, meant to feed them for the next month, disappeared into the blizzard.

His arm felt like it was being torn off as he rolled onto his belly. He kicked hard with both feet until his toes hit solid ice, only a few inches from the surface. In the blizzard a crevasse was impossible to see, the thin crust of snow like a trap door. He tried not to think of Kelly hurt. There was no movement on the line pinning him to the snow.

He levered his head up to get to the air and sucked in a breath, forcing himself to think. There were mooring spikes for the sled in his other pocket. In one complicated second, he made his sliced-up fingers grip the knife handle and used his free arm to grab them. He shoved one into the ice a couple of inches and then hammered at it with a closed fist. The oversized nail hurt his hand with every blow but his choices were the same as always – suffer or die.

He gave it five solid hits after he was sure it would take the weight then looped a scrap of rope around the top, tying it onto his belt.

One second for desperate prayer, then he undid the buckle. Kelly's line shifted and whipped a fresh groove into the snow as the spike took her weight: Roland's belt became the second link in his cobbled-together chain.

Without the weight of his partner dragging on him he felt the bones of his shoulder settle back into line again. A lesser man might have taken a few seconds to whimper and marshal his strength. Roland shoved the ground beneath him and rose to his knees.

'Kel?' he bawled into the wind. He tasted blood and swallowed it to clear his throat. He let himself slide to the edge and dug his knife into the ice at the lip as a handhold.

He saw her dangling from the safety line; it was too dark down there to see how far down the crevasse went. Maybe it was only a few feet beneath her. Maybe it went all the way to hell's hockey rink.

'Here.' Her voice shivered, eyes like shiny copper washers staring up at him.

Roland took a breath and braced his legs across the gap. She wasn't heavy, even with her pack.

For a second the strain on his arms felt good, like he'd needed to stretch and finally got the chance. But the acidic sparkle ignited his muscles quickly and he had to stop. Addicts complained that the KV robbed their strength, but Roland knew he'd sold his for another few hours drifting in blue oblivion.

'Climb up to me,' he managed.

She was a good kid, level headed and tough. But weeks of hard slog had pushed them both too far. Roland took a second to curse himself and the sadistic bastard who first mixed up a vial of KV. Even as he rested, his arms burned. His fingertips tingled with numbness as the blood froze inside his torn glove.

'I'll get the sled,' he said, the burn in his muscles forcing him to use his brain. She gave him a determined nod, finding whatever resolve she had left.

He got to his feet, made a shaky hop to the other side of the crevasse and looked around. The blizzard made Roland's world an opaque hissing blur, the white noise of wind and snowflakes driving his senses inward.

The sled had twisted sideways halfway down the slope. He got behind it and gave a shove. Pushing it uphill was twice as hard as pulling it along, but this was all he could think of to get his partner safe. Sometimes necessity was its own strength.

Each step sent electric shocks through his knees as cartilage was abraded by KV crystals. He put his shoulder into it and surged for a few jogging steps. The cold was seeping into him now; nervous sweat froze inside his clothes and numbness crept up to his wrists. His lungs pumped but got no grip on the dry air.

'Alright Kel,' he shouted down to her as he forced clumsy fingers to make a knot. 'You're tied onto the sled. You push off from the side and crawl up!'

He felt snow in his mouth: gritty and sharp, refusing to melt.

Roland offered a final prayer to whoever could hear him and shoved his weight against the sled. It only took a couple of shoves before it was sliding by itself, the wood-saw noise of the rope reeling in.

His vision slid to black from the edges, the last thing he felt was the icy world rushing up to smack him in the chest.

* * *

Kelly zipped the flap closed and returned to the sled, all the salvage pushed aside to make room for a nest of bedding and spare clothes. She checked on him.

He lay still and silent, only steam drifting from his lips indicating he was still alive. It had taken twenty minutes hugging his chest before he'd been warm enough to start shivering. You couldn't save yourself from that much cold – it took trust and teamwork, although Kelly knew it wasn't just self-preservation that made her keep saying his name and pinching his cheeks to stop him slipping away.

She'd held back the impulse to cry. To give up on him and try to conserve whatever heat was left in her tired flesh. She stared into the inside of her eyelids and listened to the wind spiralling around their tent. It paced back and forth like a bear sniffing at a hole in the ice. Kelly couldn't ignore the sound but she didn't give it credence either. He wasn't the type to just slip away in the cold. Somewhere a patient reaper followed their footprints, but no one moved over ice like Roland.

Two hours later he opened his eyes.

Kelly swiped melted frost from his face and pulled their sleeping bag snug around them both. She felt herself rise and fall a little as he took a deep breath, then another.

The cold was funny like that. Roland had seemed little more than bruised when she pulled herself up to the surface. Three steps later he'd stumbled, fallen, and when she pulled back his hood she'd thought for a moment that he was dead.

Now he was coming slowly back to life. She watched him.

Getting his awareness back, Roland saw the flimsy tent wagging in the wind above them. The memory of trying to drag Kelly up from the pit was mercifully vague, but there was little regret. They were alive. Nothing else seemed too important.

'There you are.' Kelly watched his eyes, one blue and one white, like a mongrel husky. They focused and a smile tugged at his stubbled mouth.

Kelly laughed at the look he gave her, no doubt or concern. The tough bastard looked positively smug to still be breathing. She knew how he felt.

'What's the plan Kel?' He spoke slowly, his voice a bubbling croak.

She considered. 'A lie in, I think,' she said, resting her head on his shoulder and closing her eyes.

'Good plan,' he whispered. 'Good plan.'

Victoria Floyd

Victoria Floyd is a second-year student studying English Literature at Birmingham City University. Writing is one of her biggest passions, as she believes it allows ideas and feelings to be expressed in a creative and productive way. She is inspired by everyday life, particularly from the area where she grew up – Birmingham.

Beauty and the Beast

Once upon a time, there lived a young couple. The girl was admired by all for her beauty and charm, leaving people often pondering at her choice of lover. He was the complete opposite, with a threatening stance and cruel stare.

The girl would simply tell people, 'Deep down, he is beautiful. I know he loves me.'

With her immaculate makeup, she beamed sincerity and devotion. Her lover would hold her close with showers of kisses, yet the flinch was always there. No matter how much she told people of their love, she couldn't hide the bruises.

Jack and the Beanstalk

Once upon a time, there lived a mischievous little boy. Higher and higher he would climb, gritting his teeth as he dug his tread into tree trunks.

The sky would grow closer. A bird would whistle past the boy's head: he knew no fear of heights. The wind sneaked through the boughs and around the boy's legs, threatening his balance and making his eyes water.

It seemed he could climb forever to reach the giants in the sky, until the Wicked Witch caught up with him, 'Jack, would you please get down from that tree!'

His mother abhorred his adventures.

Cinderella

Once upon a time, a young girl was in love. Her long blonde hair tumbled over her shoulders as she reached down to slip her foot into the slender heels. They were so beautiful: they appeared to be made of glass.

A sigh escaped her as she smoothed down her dress, and a smile crept across her lips. As she began to take her first steps, practicing for her place beside her lover, a hand grabbed her wrist.

'Excuse me Miss, are you going to buy those?'

Struck with sadness, she replied, 'I guess I'll have to wait until payday.'

Zoe Southall

Zoe Southall is a freelance editor, aspiring novelist, and devotee of the Oxford comma. She can often be found tending her rose garden, adding to her extensive library, or attempting to be a femme fatale. She is currently working on her first novel, a 40s style noir.

Paper and Ink

'That won't look so good when you're 60.'

Ask anyone with tattoos what the most annoying reaction to their tattoos is, and that is sure to come up a lot. I personally hate it. Imagine what you'll look like when you're 60. Short of good genetics, it's not going to be a pretty sight. I guess the point is that what looks good now won't look so good in 30, 40 years. And you're stuck with it. Forever. Wrinkly skin and wrinkly ink.

But come closer, reader. I have a confession to make. I quite like that idea.

Have you ever read Ray Bradbury's *The Illustrated Man*? You should. I first fell in love with tattoos the moment I read it. A man's tattoos come to life and predict the future. This man doesn't have ink. He has illustrations. His body is the paper to tell stories on. Isn't that a beautiful way of looking at it? The ink on your body can tell a story.

For me, my ink shows the story of my life. Milestones. Things I love. At night, I like to imagine that they come to life and complain.

'I can't breathe,' says my infinity symbol. It's on my shoulder and I often keep it covered up.

'If this girl wears another damn pair of shoes with a strap across, I'm going to poke her right on her bone.' My foot tattoo.

'I don't care. I'm a badass.' My phoenix. Then it starts singing *We Will Rock You*.

Hardly as literary as Bradbury, let's be honest. But every piece of ink has its own story. A story behind it, its meaning, what it's become.

My infinity symbol was my very first tattoo. I wanted

something small and easy to hide. It's always so hard to choose your first piece. What will it say about me? What do I love so much that I want it on my body forever? Here's another confession. I have no idea why I ended up choosing the infinity. I'm sure it meant something big and cosmic when I was 18. 'A concept that has no end and no beginning. Fabulous! I look so deep.' Fact: 18-year-olds are idiots. Most people who get the infinity have a reason – it's for a boyfriend or girlfriend. I didn't even have that excuse. Idiot. That said, I have never regretted it. It could have been a lot worse.

I got it on my 18th birthday. It would subsequently be hidden from my mother for almost a month. Like I said, idiot. But as my mum grew to accept it, it took on a different meaning for me. It's not the concept of something everlasting. It means 'always the same'. My vow to myself, back then, that nothing would ever change me. How silly is that? Time changes everyone. But it hasn't really changed the ink. It looks almost exactly the same as it did when I first showed my mum. Six years old and it's barely aged. One of the few benefits of being ghostly pale.

I made a loose sort of promise to my mum that I wouldn't get any more tattoos. I'd always wanted one and I now had it. That's what makes the second tattoo even better.

Reader, I had a breakdown. I'd go into it but it gets terribly depressing. The simple, and sad, fact is that I wasn't sure I'd survive. Then my mum made me a deal. All I had to do was get back into education. I say 'all', but that was my own version of Mission Impossible. In return, she'd pay for my next tattoo. Red flag, meet bull.

Go on any website about tattoos and they will tell you straight – getting ink on the top of your foot hurts. All tattoos hurt. Anyone who says they don't is an idiot. And any bony areas are going to hurt the most. Oh yes, it hurts, a needle tearing through your flesh. And it's visible. So it better be good. Thankfully, I couldn't be happier with it.

I wanted a quote. Something that spoke about who I was. If it's going to be visible, it better say something. Of course, that isn't always supposed to mean that it is literally readable. I had a dozen ideas. Lines from a Springsteen song. Something from *The Show Must Go On*. Something in Latin. Then I found it. It's a quote from George R.R. Martin's *A Dance with Dragons*. I can't quote it, but I can say this reader has lived many, many lives.

You don't need me to tell you that I got back into education. I got my ink. Sometimes, I like to stare at the quote and smile. I've come a long, long way since my mum and I made that deal. I wouldn't say I'm brave. But that ink gave me a lot of courage. I like to think that story would be a lot less idiotic than 'deep concept, man'. A little bit sad, but a story that gave me a reason to keep going.

Thus, I bring you to my most recent work. My phoenix. My first work is a short story. The second, a novel. The third is a song.

The first man I ever fell in love with. The moment I saw the footage of him on stage, that was it for me. He is one of the three great loves of my life. One, my library. Two, my rose garden. Three, Freddie Mercury.

I knew I wanted a third tattoo. All that stuff about only getting one? Forget it. I wanted something to commemorate two years since my breakdown. A thin excuse, yes. But what to get? I have plenty that I'm planning on. A rose for the British side of my family. A fleur de lys for the French. A lion. Another quote. A crown.

I knew I'd wanted ink as a tribute to Freddie for a while. I was seriously considering the silhouette of his statue. Then a friend suggested the phoenix. The one on the Queen logo. The same one he drew. I always have him with me now. On my shoulder, like a little angel. I think that, if it did come to life, it wouldn't speak. Not like the others. It would just start singing *The Show Must Go On*. Somehow, for Freddie and for me, it always has.

When I got the quote on my foot, the worst pain was when the tiny little 'a' was being done. I was looking at it one night, tracing it with my fingernail. And I realised something. That 'a' is very likely inked into my bone. I find that pretty wonderful. That 'a' will be there until I'm dust.

Recently, in the news, a 10,000-year-old mummy was found. And he had ink. His tattoos were still there after all those years. That ink is telling the anthropologists about his life. It's not as magical as *The Illustrated Man*. They can't speak, they can't create worlds, can't predict the future. Yet they're telling his story. Every line meant something. He didn't tell his story on paper. He told it on his skin. It's been with him for thousands of years. How incredible is that?

I can only imagine what scientists in 2000 years would think of mine. Maybe they will know about Freddie Mercury. Maybe they'll know about George R.R. Martin. I can say with almost certainty that they'll make decisions at 18 that they won't quite understand at 24. How will they know that my infinity was a strange decision? Or that my phoenix was for a man I adored? A man that died before I could ever know him? Or even that, with the help of a fantasy series, a mother's deal and some ink, I found the courage to keep going? How will they know? Because it's on my skin.

Nicky Tate

Nicky Tate has written light magazine fiction and over 200 commissioned and sponsored features for radio, frequently on educational themes. She is enjoying the challenge of extending her range through the MA Writing programme. Follow her progress at facebook.com/nickytatewriting or look and listen at nickytate.co.uk

The Challah Tin

CHAPTER ONE

His empty shop used to be a tanning salon called 'Tanfastic'. It didn't stand a chance, placed as it was next to the 50p shop, where they perpetually had three for two on tanning lotion. Or maybe it was just the High Street. It was shit and getting shitter by the month. He walked along the uneven pavement, slush soaking into the sides of his new shoes. Kenny's shop was still there, he noticed. Of course it was! Josek smiled at the thought of Kenny. Clever man. He switched to fireworks in September, Christmas lights in November and then back to laptop repair for the rest of the year. THAT'S how you did it. Kenny even tried his hand at being a barber, but a kid got an infection. Environmental health got heavy with him, so that was that. You could not *dispute* the fact that Kenny was a grafter. Josek considered himself a grafter too and the world looked after grafters. The mobile-phone-unlocking shop had gone. Shame about that. Len was nice enough and he had liked a bet too. And here was Tanfastic. Silly name. Silly girl had left it in a shameful state.

The Hawaiian beach posters in Tanfastic's window had blanched to grey. Some had fallen on the floor, to join the increasing piles of junk mail visible through the shop windows. He struggled with the door under the weight of debris behind it, and began to shove the papers into his bin bags. Passing shoppers glanced in, watching the show. He particularly enjoyed ripping off the cascading circus posters. Cheeky fuckers had inserted them through the top of the door. The sellotape attached from the outside would need cleaning off too – add it to the list. He'd left it too long to sort the place out.

Gemma had left a broom: fuchsia with zebra stripes. He chuckled, weighing it in his hands. It looked like it belonged in a bloody circus and so did he. What a fucking clown he was, pissing money away in this town. He threw the broom away, and made do scooping with his hands, on his knees.

When the rubbish was all tipped into the back bin, he moved the remaining furniture to the rear of the shop. He then wiped down the windows with pink Windolene and a soft cloth. The notice he'd printed and laminated was placed in the centre of the door, giving his details and the shop's lease terms. That might give things a boost. It bloody better. The clean smell and order comforted him, reassuring him that chaos was as temporary as you allowed it to be. In fact, he was so sure it would give things a boost that he'd reward himself with a bet. Just a small one.

It was well into the afternoon when he made it back to the cab rank. He could tell there hadn't been much trade; the *three* cabbies smoking out the front told him that. They greeted him furtively. He hated them smoking. Always leaving the tiny roll-up butts over the floor. His wife and daughter were in the back and, as per usual, made no attempt to look busy as he came in.

'She called again Papa.' This was Hana, his fat grown up daughter.

'Who?'

'Della Draper'

'She's not having it.'

Daughter turned to mother. He saw their exchanged look. Perl had been sitting smoking inside – *inside*! and reading a magazine but she put it down. They *knew*. He'd had a bet when he said he wouldn't have a bet, and he'd lost. How badly he'd lost they did not, and would never, know. Their looks to each other infuriated him. He had to quell his anger because he *knew* they would gauge the loss by the weight of his words. Once, when every penny had gone he had *almost* slapped Perl, but that was a very long time ago. She'd got driving lessons out of that one though, in the end, so there was a bright side.

'Put that fag out Perl. It's against the law now.'

He looked at his wife. Her hair irritated him. It was very short, very blonde, and flicked aggressively into a fan at the rear like a hen's backside. A fat white hen. Hana was the same – his robust little girl was now just as soft and pale, although at least she had small children to account for that. She saved her robust words for her Papa though.

'Come on Pop. A tenant's just a tenant, innit. Call her back and give her the shop.'

Josek shook his head. Irresistible frustrations surfaced.

'Middle class *wankers* moving in trying to thrust their fucking tat... *emporiums* on everyone. Pissy little candles at ten pound a go. *Ten pound!* And flags – that bunting made of cloth which is... well! Just about the least hygienic thing I've ever seen in a cafeteria.'

'We boiled the tablecloths in Krakow.' This from Perl. He nodded and pointed approvingly at his wife.

'Boiled. Every single day.' Although *she* looked boiled, he thought fleetingly, *like a boiled egg*. 'And that... that fabric bunting these cupcake people love to stick on the walls... You can't wipe it and it's collecting all the grease and fat, just *obrzydliwy. Disgusting.*'

'It's just 'kitsch' innit, Pop', said Hana. 'Bunting and cupcakes – so what if they sell a few poxy candles? People love all that shit. I mean, stuff.'

'And you should watch your language, Hana. That's why your kids are rude.'

Hana lifted her hands. It would pass as surrender, but there was something in the flick of her wrist that carried an insult. He let that one go. She then walked to the kitchen where he could hear her filling the kettle. This made him exhale heavily. Hana was a good girl.

'She only wants to sell a few cakes,' said Perl, picking up her mag again and examining the end of her extinguished cigarette.

'What on earth is wrong with that Papa? We sold cakes.'

'It wasn't *just* cakes. We sold *real* food, *traditional* food. Stuff people wanted. Stews and bread that fill your stomach. What do the displaced people in hostels up by the park want with a cupcake shop? Do you honestly think after four hours of loitering in Library... trying to keep warm, poor bastards, they think, 'do you know what I'm *gasping* for? A fucking four quid cupcake and a cup of *weak tea*.' He paused to check the colour of his own tea, as presented by Hana. It was strong.

Hana grabbed her bag and zipped up her coat. Josek noticed her coat was worn and too small. It strained over her bosom in ugly little creases. So many worries. He thought he might have a heart attack one day. He was sure of it.

'Yeah, well, Pop they didn't need a pissing tan either did they? But that didn't bother you. Just take her money! It's just a shop. You know The Cakery? Next to Primark - they do a roaring trade in all that cakey sh...tuff, and they even got wifi.'

'Oh WELL!' he roared. 'That's the clincher then, innit. Let's all go there! Matka! Get your coat on. We're going to the fucking Cakery to sit on their chilly arse benches – they've got WIFI.'

'You are just stubborn Pop. B'bye.' Hana kissed her mother and father, embracing them solidly. Josek returned the embrace. It steadied him further and he felt almost calm. As she left, a young man with a grey face came through the open door with the sleety wind, his glossy fat dog loping in behind. Josek did not like dogs. He certainly didn't like this one.

'You all right, Polish?'

'I'm OK, Mike mate. This snow is rubbish. My grandkids want to build snowmen.'

Mike could, for a moment, imagine Polish's grandkids, rosy-cheeked, lustily wading through knee-deep snow. Mike thought about his own kids, whinging about the cold after two minutes.

'You all right, Mrs P?' Her face lit up the way it always did and it didn't matter who it was. Not like his wife, thought Mike. His wife was a miserable bitch.

'We're good, Mike. You look well.'

Mike's dog circled before finding his favourite spot under the counter to lie. It occurred to Mike that Polish didn't have a dog, so his dog won.

'You see this?' Mike unfurled a flyer and laid it on the counter with a slap. 'What do you make of *that* Polish?'

'*Redcoombe in Bloom?*'

'*Flower* boxes all over, innit,' sneered Mike. It occurred to Josek that the way Mike curled his lip on the word flower was as if a flower was one of the worst swear words ever. *Flowering* bastard. *Flowering* bastard *flower*. You fucking *flower*.

'So, what's your problem? Flowers are nice. You don't like flowers?'

'Pallets of flowers. That's what the council are planning. Look at the size of the planters. Well, if they think I'm shoving a pallet of flowers in front of my offie, they can do one. How are the young mums meant to push their buggies around that? They have enough trouble with my doors as it is.'

'You still got those doors?'

'Kenny's going to sort me out new ones.'

'He better. Those prams get bigger every year, I swear.'

Josek reconsidered the content of the flyer in the light of his acquaintance's mood. He weighed the leaflet in his hands reading further to see whose idea this was. *Councillor Jafari BA (Cantab)*, Well! That was different! If this Smart Alec wanted flowers, he could go to the Esso. Just another posh boy Councillor. He patted the flyer with the back of his hand.

'This new Councillor. Never been to one of our Traders Association meetings has he?'

'Never. Fucking Joke.'

The door opened and a tall woman in a smart patterned mac

came in. Mike roused his dog and made to leave. Mike was a bigger gossip than the babushkas back home. He probably wanted to spit flowers at a few more of the traders before they closed. The woman approached the counter, sensibly giving Mike's stretching dog a wide berth.

'Hi? Are you Joe?'

Josek pointed at the sign on the wall. Joe's Minicabs. And then to himself.

'Yes, you want a cab. Perl – take this lady's details.'

'No, sorry. My name's Della Draper – I wanted to rent your shop?'

'Of course, I recognise your voice now. I'm so sorry. Like I said on the phone – it's promised already.'

Mike on his way out raised his eyebrows to Josek conveying his approval.

'I'll see you in a bit, Polish.'

Perl, beaming, appeared at his side. Josek noticed that her eyes were all over Della. Josek supposed she was judging her clothing, her jewellery, the way women did.

'Della, I'm Perl. I spoke to you this morning. Tell Joe what you have planned. It sounded really lovely. You want some tea?'

'Yes please. Look, Mr Pieniazek. At least let me show you my bank letter and my business plan. Just take a look and I won't bother you again.'

Well! Now she was going to have tea! Josek was trapped. He frowned at his wife then rubbed his forehead, glad Mike had gone. He offered Della a tiny tight smile and a head tip that was as much encouragement as she would get. She smiled and drew a slim folder from her bag. He took it and suggested she sat down. Josek was impressed at how at home she appeared to be. The sofa in the front office was too soft and everyone ended up descending a clear half-foot further than they anticipated, but she instantly readjusted herself to get comfortable. It was a terrible sofa. He really would have to ask Kenny to find him a new one.

He had known what she would look like before she had walked in. 'Well off.' She was tall, and pretty too but looked hard, from the angles of her tailored coat to the cut of her hair. The glossy raincoat with the maroon pattern was cut in the way those fashionable clothes were. It seemed to have big tucks and creases in odd places; you thought it was a mistake but they were there on purpose. That's probably what his wife had been looking at. Though hard, she did not look weathered. The hardness was more like shiny glass than concrete.

Josek opened her folder on the counter and turned the pages looking at each one for the very bare minimum amount of time. He made no effort to break the silence. He had no need to make this an easy conversation for her. Perl placed the tea on the coffee table and snaked into the backroom where a phone had actually started to ring. Irritatingly, Della wasn't squirming in her seat.

She sipped her tea and smiled at him. 'You only put that notice up today Joe.' There was something in her direct tone which he would have found impertinent in his wife or daughter.

'Yes. I put it up today – so what?'

He knew she couldn't read his face. His words were more likely to give him away and he could ration those with ease.

More silence. He turned back a few pages for the look of it, out of politeness, as if he needed to check some detail. Glancing up, he saw she was scrutinising him. *Now he saw it!* She probably figured that if she waited long enough he'd say more words, do more things and she'd have more pieces for her puzzle. He read people too but *no one* could do silence better than a Pieniazek. He smiled to himself as he remembered Hana as a teenager. She could make an aria out of a silence and a slammed door. Of course, Della cracked first. She placed her cup with both hands on the table. Knight to King Four.

'Come on Joe, help me out here', she urged. *She was as familiar with him as if she was family!* 'Maybe you can remember trying to get your first shop, maybe someone did you a favour?'

The way she was smiling at him, eyes connecting directly with his, she almost – yes he was sure, she appeared to be *flirting* a little, or at least attempting to. She was a very beautiful woman. Or maybe she was just thin. He'd not shared silence with anyone this beautiful so close-up since his mother had died and a nurse had held his hand. He looked at *her* hands, not remotely hiding his gaze. No ring. He tried to remember if she had been a Mrs in the letter she'd sent him. Maybe there was a husband bankrolling her. If his wife looked like this, he'd bankroll her.

'There are precious few favours in business. You should know that Della.'

'But there are some. For people you know, I bet.'

'I don't know you Della. Look, there are plenty of other shops empty, why mine?'

'Yours has decent flooring. And it's clean.' Josek was pleased she'd noticed the flooring. He'd paid extra for it at the time. These days it would be lino. He returned to her papers. One page was all about her Internet shop. *Internet shop!*

'Pah. See here! You can't run a proper business on the Internet.'

'Of course you can. You think I made up those figures? I'll be stuck in cyberspace if I can't find a shop, though. Won't I?' He smiled, reassured that he was still in charge. She smiled back, appealing to him with familiar eyes. Josek relaxed a little. It was a pity, in some respects this conversation had to be short, and then she would go. He liked the way she was focused so *intently* on him.

When he was a younger (much younger) man in Poland, he'd seen the movie *Lawrence of Arabia* with Peter O'Toole and Omar Sharif at the black market cinema on the Tomasza. As many films were in those days, it was a long film but it went too fast. Josek was strongly moved by the heroism and humanity and the lavish scenery. Deserts and bleaching sun about as far as you could get from rationing and riots and all the other nonsense that made him glad to leave Poland. He had felt bereft emerging from the dark room on that one day, however, walking back into the comparative light of the drab streets that characterised the Old Town. A year later he was able to absorb the detail at his leisure having acquired the book *The Seven Pillars of Wisdom*, and this gave him satisfaction.

This conversation with Della was like a movie – little lines running past; glances and silences. He could almost hear the music for the title credits. He wished he owned the book of Della so that he could linger over her at his leisure. He wondered what it would be like to sleep with her. He ached a little, this thought giving him an emptying pang because *that* would never happen and their conversation suddenly felt stupid because it wasn't truthful. She spoke.

'You do kind of know me a bit. My mum says she used to work for you years ago – at your café? Selina?'

Josek pouted, he couldn't have looked less interested if she'd told him she was wearing a maroon coat or was drinking tea. He answered, resigned to untruthfulness.

'We had a lot of staff. I don't remember.'

Carrier: An Excerpt

INT. GREEN HOUSE ACADEMY CORRIDOR — DAY

We can hear children chanting a bright but severe
song in Mandarin Chinese. SARAH and ANDREA are
walking along a corridor, holding papers and
talking a little conspiratorially.

>   SARAH
>   He's still got my phone… I mean why
>   would he do that? Wasn't he, like,
>   weird about the whole thing?
>
>   ANDREA
>   Come on, you know what he's like.
>   Total. Control. Freak. He's just going
>   to claim all the credit for what Bobby's
>   done and he'll be the Academy poster boy
>   for the next, like, HUNDRED years.

They laugh. ANDREA turns to enter her classroom.
A teaching assistant is animatedly singing the
severe song in Mandarin Chinese with the children.
She meets ANDREA'S gaze cheerily and continues the
song.

>   ANDREA
>   See you later.

Some black people-carriers are pulling up outside.
They're visible through the wall-to-ceiling thick
glass windows of ANDREA'S classroom.

>   ANDREA
>   Hey, what's all THAT about…?

INT. ANDREA'S CLASSROOM — DAY

SARAH moves into the classroom, and she and ANDREA move towards the thick windows to see what's going on. The children continue to chant severely. SHEP can be seen carrying a child towards the waiting cars.

It's BOBBY. He's not wearing a coat or shoes.

                    SARAH
          Hey, is that Bobby? What the…

A suited woman steps out of the back of one car and receives BOBBY. She is expressionless and brisk. BOBBY squirms. SHEP glances about, nervous.

SARAH runs to the glass and bangs on it, shouting with increasing urgency. The chanting children drown her out. ANDREA joins her at the window. BOBBY sees SARAH and reaches out his arms, bewildered.

                    SARAH
          SHEP!   SHEP!   BOBBY!

                    ANDREA
          What the hell? Get out there — go on
          Sarah — look! They're going!

SARAH runs out of the classroom. ANDREA bangs and waves at SHEP who is in conversation with someone in the front of one of the cars. The car doors and windows slam, BOBBY inside.

INT. GREEN HOUSE ACADEMY CORRIDOR — DAY

SARAH sprints furiously down the long corridor, her feet hammering on the tile. The chanting song is still audible.

EXT. GREEN HOUSE ACADEMY — DAY

SARAH arrives outside too late as the cars speed
off. SHEP instantly attempts to pacify SARAH.

> SHEP
> We're just worried Sarah, they think
> Bobby might be in danger.

> SARAH
> WHO thinks Bobby's in danger — Who were
> they? Where the hell are they taking my
> son, Shep?

SHEP looks embarrassed and anxious and attempts to
calm SARAH by holding her arms — she shoves his
hands off her.

A Police Car pulls up.

> SHEP
> It's Viroport. They think Bobby might
> have been infected with something.

> SARAH
> Bobby's never even BEEN to Viroport!
> Where's my son? Where IS HE?

> SHEP
> I'm sorry. He's safe. Look, they'll
> take you to him now.

SARAH staggers, reeling. A kindly looking
policeman helps her into the back of the police
car. It drives away, wheels spinning in the
gravel. SHEP is left looking lost.

INT. A POLICE CELL — DAY

SARAH is led into a police cell, all the time
being reassured by the police officer.

> POLICE OFFICER
> We just need you to wait here for us,
> for a moment. Please don't worry about
> Bobby. He's in good hands.

She tries to interrupt but he leaves and the door
shuts. She realises she's imprisoned.

                    SARAH
        Excuse me? EXCUSE ME! What's going on?
        I NEED TO KNOW WHERE MY SON IS!

No response. She looks about fearfully and
doesn't know where to put herself. Gasping in
sobs, she huddles on the bench.

INT. A STARK DIVIDED ROOM AT VIROPORT - DUSK

Low light in a clinical room at Viroport. The room
contains a hospital style bed with BOBBY, now
asleep but huddled. He is small, and naked under
a white sheet. His hand is bandaged.

Two laboratory assistants are working with a row
of vials of blood. They can see BOBBY through a
large adjoining window. One tests with a pipette,
the other makes notes on a computer.

                    LAB ASSISTANT 1
        Sample 23 TAU-CETI-4 positive.

                    LAB ASSISTANT 2
        Check — sample 23 TAU-CETI-4 positive.
        Should we phone them now?

LAB ASSISTANT 2 eyes a clinical pack of three
syringes in a secure translucent case. They are
named SODIUM THIOPENTAL, PANCURONIUM BROMIDE and
POTASSIUM CHLORIDE. They are criss-crossed with
HAZARDOUS stickers on them.

                    LAB ASSISTANT 1
        There's no requirement unless the
        majority of samples come through
        positive. And we wouldn't be expected to
        do that anyway.

LAB ASSISTANT 2 is younger, softer. She looks

anxiously at the sleeping child. She sniffs,
blinks firmly and returns to the vials.

LAB ASSISTANT 1

Sample 24 positive for TAU-CETI-4.

INT. A POLICE CELL — DUSK

Fluorescent lights switch on with a zipping
noise. SARAH is still perched in exactly the same
position, hugging herself.

Her face is tear-streaked. She hears footsteps
and rushes to the tiny grille. Keys rattle and
the door is unlocked.

INT. SARAH'S HOUSE — NIGHT

SARAH opens the door, clicks on a light and makes
directly for the landline telephone.

Grabbing the cordless receiver and cradling it
in her neck, she searches through the papers on
the side table for CHARIE'S card, swearing. She
upends the pile, scrabbling on the floor.

SARAH

Please… please…

She's GOT it! She dials.

INT. DESPERATELY HIP BAR — NIGHT

CHARLIE'S on what appears to be a date with a
PRETTY GEEK.

She's nerdy and cool-retro but the chemistry is a
little uncomfortable because the PRETTY GEEK is
far, far too young for Charlie. What's more she's
tipsy and will not shut up.

CHARLIE is politely smiling at her monologue but
glazing over.

> PRETTY GEEK
>
> So we sent out these crazy videos but we hid these algorithms in them and you had to like watch the whole thing, and piece together the clues, and all the lads were like — make it a cat, 'cause everyone loves a cat video but I thought that was well shit because it would just get lost in like a zillion cat videos and would never go viral…

> CHARLIE
> (interrupting…)
>
> …Yeah, when you said you were into viruses…?

> PRETTY GEEK
>
> …Viral marketing yeah.

> CHARLIE
> (the penny drops…)
>
> …*Right.*

> PRETTY GEEK
>
> So like we got these mad web animators to make the cat turn into a monkey but if you clicked on his eyes…

RING! CHARLIE'S mobile jolts him back into reality. Glancing down to see who's calling — it's SARAH.

He holds up a finger and dazzles a smile at the PRETTY GEEK who yabbers on, regardless.

> CHARLIE
> (mouthing to her silently)
>
> *Need to take this — one minute? 'k?*

He stands up and edges away. It's too loud to hear. He breaks into a jog towards the door market TOILETS.

INTERCUT:

> SARAH
>
> Charlie you've got to help me, something
> weird is going on, they've taken Bobby.
> They think he has some virus… They've
> taken my phone…

INT. DESPERATELY HIP BAR CORRIDOR — NIGHT

It's quieter in the corridor. CHARLIE is listening
to SARAH on the phone and is shocked at what he
hears.

> CHARLIE
>
> You what? WHO'S taken him?

INTERCUT:

> SARAH
>
> Shep just handed him over to some guys
> from Viroport and they say they're
> running tests, I mean can they even DO
> that?

> CHARLIE
>
> Look are you OK? Physically? Alright.
> You're at home now? I'm coming straight
> over. It's OK, we'll figure it out.

CHARLIE hangs up.

Charlotte McDermott

Charlotte McDermott is a twenty-year-old under-graduate and an aspiring writer, studying English and Creative Writing. She enjoys all forms of writing, but poetry in particular. She is a lively and friendly individual, which contrasts directly with the themes she chooses to write about. Number one procrastinations include playing Internet games, watching *Doctor Who* and listening to *Walk Off The Earth*. Eventually, she wants to go into publishing and editing, including publishing her own works.

Amphibian's Amphitheatre

Suspended in tree leaves within the heart
Of the prince-frog's forest, eyes from all sides;
The all-watchers, all-waiters, worlds apart
From these creatures, but the real beast resides
In stasis, amidst the darkest reaches;
A place within us where no light breaches.
One kiss wakes the fabled prince from slumber;
From magician to lover, his saviour,
All seems well inside his world asunder –
A double life, one of misbehaviour,
So false pretences shroud the slit-eyed soul;
The vertebrate reveals his heart-shaped hole.
The magic fades amidst his stage of smog;
The prince recedes now, back into a frog.

The Old Sakura Tree

In the open field of rolling hills and crisp vermillion grasses,
The branches of the old sakura tree lie bare
Through the long winter months and the longer wisps of
    icy wind,
As it weaves throughout the valleys
And through the blades of grass,
Until they collide with the old sakura tree.

We sit together, side-by-side,
Warming our bodies in the bitter winter air,
Sitting atop the hillside, opposite naked growth,
Watching,
Waiting.

Spring creeps through into the air,
Warming our bones – so we shuffle from one another.
The old sakura tree, she blossoms.
In a hue of pale pink the leaves grow from mother sunlight,
Filling and flooding the hillside with flits
Of contrasting colour to the norm: we observe.

Time wears on, wind returns to claim his forgotten territory,
Until the leaves on the old sakura tree
Sweep gracefully through the space around us;
Upon the floor, mid-air, in your raven hair.

Like the leaves on the trees we blossomed, love appeared,
Love wrapped us in her arms and held us tight,

I kissed you under the stars.
Like the leaves on the trees we wilted, love disappeared,
Flew through the air and quietly vanished.
The wind swept our love away, into the night,
Past the old sakura tree.

Intermingled Misfortunes:
Alexander Pushkin and Eugene Onegin

He is not a lover, who does not love forever - *Euripides*

1
A creature crafted from his pen,
Pushkin wrote of a loveless man;
The passions of his heart could then
Lay dormant, nothing left to span
The empty spaces of his soul,
So life no longer took its toll
On poor Onegin, feelings meek,
His view on life was very bleak.
The character was popular,
He entertained with a small crowd,
Some were ladies, some were men proud
To be so rounded, circular,
But pride is a consuming sin –
In a duel only one can win.

2
Pushkin wrote of both love and loss –
Eugene, he loved, and Eugene lost
His dear friend Lensky, who would toss
His life away, the highest cost
For the poor man to pay for pride;
His best friend Eugene never cried.
He wasn't one for social balls,
But Lensky lied, so friendship falls;
By flirting with Lensky's fair wife
Onegin took his cruel revenge,
So Lensky set out to avenge
His hurt conceit, not with a knife,
But with a pistol duel at dawn,
And leaves the world with friends forlorn.

3
Pushkin wasn't very different,
He had the fairest wife in hand
Natalya was radiant,
The fairest maiden of the land.
Even the Tsar of Russia had
A flare for Pushkin's wife, but sad
Was Pushkin not, 'til d'Anthès
Crept out from his rock in Alsace.
A wealthy, martial man was he,
Born a lover to his bones;
Through letters to his 'father'* groans,
He craved, he wanted Natalie,
"This love poisons my existence."
Georges clung to his resistance.

4
"The secret belongs only to
[H]er and to me."[2] To Heeckeren wrote
And confessed did he, but just through
Letters and glances could they float
In dreams, no more than face value;
She was stuck to her spouse like glue.
Yet it was no secret, his love,
Wild with envy was Pushkin thereof.
For some time did he pine for her,
But Georges was driven away;
Although despite fixation, nay,
Obsession, his actions differed:
Her sister, Ekaterina,
Did he court for a cortina**.

*Heeckeren, d'Anthes' adoptive father

**A cortina is a cobweb-like veil

5

Pushkin, "always melancholy,
[A]bstracted and worried"[3] was he,
Rapt by Georges gaze unholy
Towards his precious Natalie.
D'Anthès pleaded her to leave
Her Pushkin, attempted to thieve
Her from his side, he did not know
Back then the omen he did sow.
Writing to his father once more,
The rejected fan did suffer,
"(I) began to weep," he did transfer,
"[L]ike a great fool," Georges did roar.
Gone "mad with mental suffering"[4],
D'Anthes had to be her king.

6

"He was dying of love for her"[5],
A fool for love d'Anthès was,
Now nothing short of a stalker,
The crazed and frenzied follower has
Threatened to take a pistol to
His own skull and bid them all adieu,
Should she not give herself to him,
But she escaped and left him grim.
You must have wondered where he's gone,
The name man, the 'biographee';
Alexander, by Natalie,
Was ultimately informed on
The subject of the desperate man,
His surplus love and his failed plan.

7

Never doubted for an instant
Natalya's sweet innocence[6].
Never wavered for a moment,
Creating that omen ambiance;
A cartel and his judgment sent,
His love and will were both hell-bent:
Georges and he would duel to death,
'Til one of them breathes their last breath.
Viewed by some, his peers and brothers,
Our poet Pushkin, tired of life,
Had used this duel to rid his strife
(But Natalie would be no others);
"To put a bullet through his head,
His former love of life was dead."[7]

8

The courted sister, the scapegoat,
Ekaterina was the key;
Prevent the sailing of that boat,
The duel for them to drown in seas
Of vain bloodshed, a firing gun,
Taking lives in the sake of one.
D'Anthès would wed her sister,
But Pushkin felt this sore blister
Under his skin; a noted lie,
In order to prevent the duel.
This merely gave the fire a fuel;
He could not rest – the man must die –
He daren't be cheated of his prey[8]
For Pushkin's heart was in dismay.

9

The rumours did not help the strife,
"They say in society that
D'Anthès is courting my wife.
Some say she likes him, others that
She doesn't." [9] Pushkin did explain,
Although it must have caused him pain.
To find a second was a deed
That had to be done with some speed.
Poor Pushkin, he did struggle here,
For no man seemed a worthy hand
To stand by him in his last stand,
So in the end no one came near;
D'Anthès crafty plot to wed
Avoided bullets made of lead.

10

Lying heroically, Georges
Said that Natalya was a
Mere go-between:[10] Pushkin's hinges
Were unscrewed; life was looking grey.
The stubborn poet did refuse
To have d'Anthès family fused;
Pushkin would not dare receive
The scoundrel that would plain deceive
His friends and peers, just to avoid
The barrel of his new foe's gun,
But soon d'Anthès would not run
Away from bonds he had destroyed;
D'Anthès was the Eugene and
Our Pushkin was the Lensky grand.

11

After an exchange of letters,
Some of which addressed to him
Were dispersed throughout the fetters
Of their small society prim,
Alexander, made a fool of,
Refused to let go of his love
For Natalya; he refused
To stand down, for his heart was bruised.
No vicious rumour, tempting lie,
Nor truth displaced could blind him hence
From all the years he's spent from whence
She appeared and caught his keen eye.
A love enduring and thus strong,
Could only last for ever long.

12

This is where the story differs,
For Eugene could not woo his love;
Long had she loved him, next she butters
Up his heart, and like a warm glove
Slides in, and fits, and sits, and stirs
His tepid heart, becoming hers.
Too late was he, the poet's knight,
Tatyana had already plight
In marriage to a noble heir.
Past years gone by, Eugene had lost
A beauty, carelessly he'd tossed,
Leaving Onegin to despair
And pine for love he could've had;
Emotions that can drive you mad.

13

Tatyana, though she loved him dear,
Could never break her marriage bond,
Instead she let her yearning peer
Love on in vain and she beyond
All reason of her own remains
A faithful wife, despite her pains.
Let us hope that our dear poet –
For he did love, that he knew it –
Was not akin to Tanya's beau;
A man, though blessed with marriage could
Have been a loveless man for good,
Devoted to by morals, though
She truly loved another still,
And fought this love with all her will.

14

Though Pushkin doubted not his wife,
But of the duel, it was deferred;
As though he'd waited all his life,
The fire in his stomach stirred.
The whole event had taken now
A toll so evident and ploughed
On right through the poet's preaches;
Farouche and silent were his speeches,
Broken only by staccato,
Brief, and ironic words, devilish
And demonic laughter[11]; cherished
Once his aching heart, vibrato
Now the rapid beats do vary,
When d'Anthès makes him weary.

15

D'Anthès beloved father
Tried his finest to patch the rift
(Though he may well not have bothered)
Between the kin that were adrift;
D'Anthès and Natalya
So they say was history, a
Letter sent to Pushkin's door
Was thrown back in his face with scorn,
"You shall take it [back], you scoundrel!"
Destroying hopes of compromise,
All were useless in Pushkin's eyes,
Continuing the fatal quarrel.
Although the duel he did withdraw,
His icy malice was not thawed.

16

Pushkin believed her chastity,
But d'Anthès proved a fool again,
He danced with joy with Natalie;
Georges existence was his bane.
"Natalya had unburdened
[H]er heart to him and [now] he had
[R]esolved to act… on the morrow"[12];
Georges, once more, cursed tomorrow.
One of Pushkin's loyal friends,
Found him dining "happy, free
[F]rom those mental sufferings" he
Was long tortured by to no ends.
This was despite the fact that he
Again was set to duel, not flee.

17

Pushkin could not find a second,
Much like his Eugene Onegin;
Eugene never even reckoned
That the duel was worth it wherein
The great matter that was at hand;
Our Eugene couldn't understand.
He was not stern or serious,
And was always mysterious;
He arrived a full hour late,
Much to Lenky's second's anger,
And yet there was no cliff-hanger,
Straight to the duel with no restraint;
Zaretsky never realised
The cost of what the duel comprised.

18

Long-standing friendship did combine
With honour, and the poet's friend,
Danzas, could surely not decline
The offer, though it was his end.
The seconds signed the protocol –
Twenty paces, with a pistol,
One shot only was to be fired,
No position change should conspire,
With no result they will repeat,
Until one adversary's shot.
Commandant's villa, five o'clock,
Would be the place of deathly feat.
Guns "made in Paris, by Lepage"[13] –
Another Onegin homage.

19

They travelled, passing Natalie,
Collecting the Pushkin children,
Fortunately she did not see,
And to his death called the siren.
Our hero Pushkin turned and aimed
But Georges cheated unashamed;
D'Anthès was a pace away
And lived to see another day.
Pushkin fell, shot in the spleen,
His sacrum shattered, in the bone
The ball was lodged, but with a groan
Pushkin now took his shot so clean;
It should've killed the swindling foe,
But missed, struck below the elbow.

20

All hope was lost and two days on,
Natalya did despair;
Alexander Pushkin was gone
And his wife's heart was now laid bare,
Stripped of happy, joyful feeling,
For in her sadness she was reeling,
Draped in guilt and clothed in sorrow,
No more cause to wake tomorrow,
She threw herself onto her knees
And put her face into his own[14].
It was for her his life he'd thrown
Away, for love, for life, for peace.
He died for love, ne'er diminished,
"Life is finished, life is finished."[15]

Endnotes

1. Binyon, T. J., *Pushkin A Biography*, 2002, *A Sea of Troubles*, p. 521

2. Binyon, T. J., *Pushkin A Biography*, 2002, *A Sea of Troubles*, p. 521

3. Binyon, T. J., *Pushkin A Biography*, 2002, *The Final Chapter*, p. 547

4. Binyon, T. J., *Pushkin A Biography*, 2002, *The Final Chapter*, p. 555

5. Binyon, T. J., *Pushkin A Biography*, 2002, *The Final Chapter*, p. 557

6. Binyon, T. J., *Pushkin A Biography*, 2002, *The Final Chapter*, p. 561

7. Pushkin, Alexander, *Eugene Onegin*, 1825-1832, 1833, stanza 38, p. 22

8. Binyon, T. J., *Pushkin A Biography*, 2002, *The Final Chapter*, p. 570

9. Binyon, T. J., *Pushkin A Biography*, 2002, *The Final Chapter*, p. 582

10. Binyon, T. J., *Pushkin A Biography*, 2002, *The Final Chapter*, p. 585

11. Binyon, T. J., *Pushkin A Biography*, 2002, *The Final Chapter*, p. 600

12. Binyon, T. J., *Pushkin A Biography*, 2002, *The Final Chapter*, p. 611

13. Binyon, T. J., *Pushkin A Biography*, 2002, *The Final Chapter*, p. 621

14. Binyon, T. J., *Pushkin A Biography*, 2002, *The Final Chapter*, p. 630

15. Binyon, T. J., *Pushkin A Biography*, 2002, *The Final Chapter*, p. 630

David Roberts

David Roberts's biography of Thomas Betterton was short-listed for the Theatre Library Association's George Freedley Award in 2011. Now he's writing a further book for Cambridge University Press. He has also published five books with Oxford University Press and writes programme essays for the Royal Opera House. He would love someone to take an interest in his first novel, *A Hellish Plot*.

Family History

For a long time I relied on guesswork. I didn't know if there had ever been a photograph of her, or whether one had survived, or if it was there all the time, nestling in the unsorted boxes in my mother's loft. So I pieced her together as best I could.

Other family faces told the best story. Medium build, dark brown hair somewhere between wavy and curly, naturally healthy. Probably, the appendage known to my own children as 'the Briggs nose'– a blobby, uneven growth prone to spots and moles, although she wouldn't have had time to develop and then regret it. Brown eyes, surely. Her jaw would have been slender, her chin small and her teeth crooked. In time, her hair would have resisted greying. She would have matured into heart trouble; her bones would have grown brittle and her eyesight grainy. Above all, she would have been dutiful to the last. A willing bearer of messages my Aunt Barbara must have been – a keen sergeant on any mission.

One certainty towered over all my guesses. In 1936, when she was eleven and my mother just turned ten, she died.

It happened at a level crossing near to home, my mother said. Early morning, and I'd always supposed she must have been on her way to school. I pictured the girl running with her bag, squeezing under the barrier as a dare, or just looking the wrong way and somehow failing to hear the oncoming train. The scene blended readily into my own childhood, spent in a house next to a railway line that used to carry me to school every day, past several level crossings where Barbara's death occasionally acquired a new backdrop, different kinds of weather: now, a freezing morning with the train looming out of the fog and the girl's foot slipping on a patch of ice; then again, a dreary, rain-swept day when waiting for the barrier to rise meant getting drenched on the way to double maths or geography; sometimes, just a dazzling spring day, with daffodils blooming and a life abruptly over.

It was a school day, but only for my mother. She was called out of class, and the headmistress told her that her sister was dead. At the end of the day, at home, came two more discoveries. Unable to bear telling her the news directly, her parents had left instructions with school that they should do it. That summary explanation out of the way, they forbade my mother ever to mention the subject again. There would be no discussion, no further account of what happened, no mention of her sister in their presence. Only then would they – *all* of them – be able to deal with the terrible event. The girl had died at a level crossing, and that was that.

And that, I supposed for a while, was why my mother said nothing more to me about my Aunt Barbara, and why I never saw her photograph. Until recently, that is.

Reading, as well as the school train, filled out the gaping spaces of the story. I imagined the scene from *David Copperfield* where David learns of his mother's death:

> '*When you came to School, your sister was not with you.*'
>
> *My mother trembled, without distinctly knowing why, and looked earnestly at the headmistress, making no attempt to answer.*
>
> '*Because,*' *said the headmistress,* '*I grieve to tell you that I hear this morning your sister has had an accident.*'
>
> *A mist rose between the headmistress and my mother, and her figure seemed to move in it for an instant. Then my mother felt the burning tears run down her face.*
>
> '*Your sister Barbara has been very badly hurt,*' *she added.*

My mother knew everything now.
'She is dead.'
There was no need for the headmistress to say so.
My mother had already broken out into a desolate cry.

Surely, I reasoned, she discussed it with Leslie, her brother, who would adopt the name of Rick ('such an unmanly name, Leslie,' my mother explained). From the way she talked about him after his death, it was easy to see how she loved him, but they'd had their own breach. When my grandmother died, they argued bitterly over the will. There was one furious row over the phone – a shocking eruption into the glacial stillness of life at home. Leslie, a war hero who had been a navigator on Mosquito bombers, cut a dashing, Brylcreamed figure and had married a glamorous woman with, I just recall, dark hair in a sixties beehive. He had fallen into a job that allowed him to rub shoulders with the rich and famous: some sort of assistant to a film producer who introduced him to stars and paid him in used notes.

They had made up, Leslie and my mother, after his wife died. My mother had been shocked to see him waiting for the reunion in our front porch, yellow from smoking, purple from brandy. But the old intimacy had soon returned. 'Your mum was very upset,' my father confided afterwards, his tone forestalling further mention.

So it had always been possible to imagine to see how the two of them, Leslie and my mother, might have coped in 1936 and for years afterwards, exchanging memories of their sister while their parents sat downstairs in the gloom, listening to the grandfather clock in the hall, terrified of *that* subject coming up. The same soft footprint dented my own consciousness of the story until last year. Believing in it just as it stood, asking no further questions, seemed the right thing to do. It was an article of faith, of respect for the old white family scar. But one Thursday evening my wife, who'd heard the story often, declared she had always been suspicious.

'In fact,' she said, stirring a curry round in the frying pan, 'I never believed it at all.'

'Oh?'

'Think about it,' she said, leaving the dish to stand and turning to me.

Killed at a level crossing? Too easy – especially when my grandfather was a station master. The station master's daughter killed at a level crossing: its very plausibility gave the game away. Something worse had happened that he'd explained away with the comfortingly obvious – so obvious that it need never be mentioned again. Surely the most repressed family could cope with the idea of an accident on the railway, especially when they worked next to one.

'Otherwise why should they have been so keen not to talk about it?' she asked.

'Generational thing? People felt differently then.'

She pulled a face.

'Not that differently.'

And she turned off the heat and began to serve.

The great empty spaces of the story now filled up with a more lurid kind of fiction: something shameful, monstrous, unspeakable had taken place. A child molester who had turned to violence; a kidnapper; suicide, even. At the very least, there was something to investigate. The most sensational eventuality of all lay beckoning at the end of the trail – that somewhere, perhaps far away on another continent, my Aunt Barbara was still alive. I started to dream of tracking her down and, after seventy years, reuniting her with my mother.

Before I had any facts to go on, there was no point broaching the subject with my mother. She had fallen ill, and I began to wonder if she would live to hear the truth about Barbara, or whether it

might kill her. At the slightest allusion to the story I could feel
the cryogenic misery of decades past, hear the hatches batten-
ing. I started to trawl the Internet. Local newspaper archives
were no use. I sidestepped the commercial family history sites
and went for registers of births, marriages and deaths. My
mother was raised in Macclesfield, and it was not long before I
found Barbara Briggs, born in the East Cheshire district in 1925,
a year before my mother. Her grandfather I also found; he had
died three years before Barbara was born.

But then there was a blank. Joseph Briggs had been a
Macclesfield station master. Of Barbara Briggs's death, which I'd
always been told had happened so close to home, there was no
record in the Cheshire register. I tried each district – nothing.
The gap beckoned, and I fantasized about an unrecorded death.
The abduction – the girl gone missing – the parents' cover-up for
their confused surviving daughter. I envisaged a scene in which
I would confront my mother with this stark, terrible truth: there
was no evidence that her sister had died. Perhaps, after so many
decades' absence, she was still alive somewhere, just.

Then an answer, of sorts. It was different from my wilder imag-
inings, but also from the story my mother had told me. Barbara
Briggs, died in December 1936, not at Macclesfield, but at
Stone, aged eleven. She even had a reference number, her name
snug in the top left-hand corner of the registry of the dead
for Staffordshire. For twenty pounds – a small price for a big
denouement – and a delay of four to five weeks, I could order a
copy of the death certificate. I clicked the button and dropped an
email to my brother Ian.

His reply was not long in coming. Had he too caught the non-
speaking bug? When I looked again at his message, it seemed so.
There was a woman in his village who had lost a child decades
ago and never got over it; Barbara was too difficult a topic to
broach with our mother, who had never spoken of her to him

apart from giving the bare outline of the story. It was characteristic of Ian. At our father's post mortem it turned out that the heart attack which killed him had a predecessor whose damage lurked in his arteries. We both knew it had happened when he had fallen downstairs in a faint the year before and then brusquely denied it. The doctor, a locum in a hurry, had told him to take more care and promptly departed. I was adamant that our mother should know the result of the post mortem; Ian was equally adamant that she should not. 'What right have we to know when she doesn't?' I had asked. Eventually, he'd given in and when I told her she seemed surprised, but glad to know. When I said I wanted to ask her if she knew where Barbara had really died, he said no.

'What would be the point?' he asked, and I wasn't sure.

He need not have worried. One week before the certificate turned up, my mother died. Ian was right. I'm glad now that I never had the chance to tell her the real story.

Expecting the brown envelope for weeks, I somehow managed to leave it lying in a pile of papers for a day or so before I realised what it was. I picked it up, held it for a moment and slit the envelope open with a paring knife, anxious to avoid damage. Then I pulled out the certificate, put the knife down, unfolded the paper, and began to read.

The spidery hand of the Staffordshire coroner had recorded, with pitying formality, that 'unfortunately this young lady died attempting to traverse the level crossing at Stone.' No monsters, then, no melodrama – just an accident, a train looming out of the fog and a girl's foot slipping on the ice. Joseph Briggs, Station Master at Macclesfield; Irene Briggs, his wife; and their loss. But the coroner had not finished. He had another sentence to bestow on Joseph and Irene, and it was for life: for their lives, for my mother's life, and now for mine.

Trailing along the bottom of the certificate, the cramped ink spelled out the mystery of why she had died at Stone:

'It seems this young lady was sent by her parents on an errand, which she was sadly unable to complete.'

Darker shapes now filled the deserts of the story: the crying shadows of Joseph and Irene Briggs, my grandparents, tortured to silence by their self-reproach. No wonder they forbade my mother to speak of it. She might never have stopped.

A month after my mother died, I found a box of photographs in the far corner of her loft. Beneath a pile of photographs of Leslie in his uniform, Leslie smoking a cigarette on an Italian beach, Leslie pouring a glass of wine, I found a crumpled picture of the figure of a child like my mother but strangely altered. Medium build, dark brown hair somewhere between wavy and curly, naturally healthy. The appendage known to my own children as 'the Briggs nose'. Brown eyes, surely. Her jaw slender, her chin small and her teeth crooked. A dependable air, a girl you could rely on. A willing bearer of messages, my Aunt Barbara was; a keen sergeant on any mission.

Now, whenever the train I'm on rushes past a level crossing, I half expect to see her, ducking below the barrier amid the thundering din. She's never there, of course. But sometimes, half through tears, I think I see Joseph and Irene, running up the lane, calling out to their child, desperate to unsay the message they had given her that morning.

Daniel Wilkes

Daniel Wilkes is a soon to be English graduate currently based in Birmingham. He is a lover of the strange and firmly believes good science fiction does exist... somewhere. Outside of his writing he is researching the philosophy of the mind and wild ideas such as physicalism and substance dualism.

Entropy

I
PETRA: THE WASTE

A silver tempest laced with lightning thrashes through the waste.

Frosted shards fizz, hum and splinter into the rock ribbed landscape.

A ballet of chaos.

Virgil weaves through the storm.

Her ivory hair lingers behind.

She keeps running, her pink eyes set nowhere but ahead.

Virgil is swatted aside by a raging squall.

Immense silver shards of sky splinter and are cast in the storm.

They fly and fizz and fall all around her and hunt Virgil like the arrows of Artemis.

One slices her white robe at the shoulder.

   She bleeds.

Raw sanguine throbs and spreads down the sleeve.

No grimace or wince at the injury. Survival is her only focus.

   LIGHTNING.

A sovereign strike fractures the floor ahead.

It begins to jaw apart and slip away.

   She pushes on.

Harder.

   Digging deeper.

And leaps over the void.

Her arms flail and paddle the air.

Virgil lands with a crunch. What breath she had is lost.

She pulls herself up and sprints up the slipping incline.

The soil is rolling down from the apex of the rock.
Her feet struggle to climb the tipping rock.
An immeasurable silver spike spears into the top of the sinking rock.
It counterbalances the weight, tipping VIRGIL the other way.
The rock groans with the weight shift and cracks again.
Another chunk of silver plows into the rock she hangs on.
The storm has arrived.
Virgil hangs by an arm from her tilting rock.
The sediment is oscillating violently.
A slip of the arm…
Virgil

      Sssssl-

      iii…

-pps away…
And tumbles into the void.
Everything lost in her infinite wail.
CUT TO BLACK.

II
PETRA: CAVE

Drip.
Black.
Drip.
Panting.
Drip.
Shuffling.
Drip.
Light sweats in, somewhere from the left.
Drip.
Virgil's chalky robe is illuminated.
Drip.

She limps into the retreating darkness.

Drip.

Drip.

Virgil is an ivory spectre dancing through the dark.

Drip.

Drip.

III
PETRA: UNDERGROUND LAKE

A vast aquamarine lake, boundless in size.

    It swells and exhales an azure aurora.

Virgil is awestruck.

A thin peninsula leads through the lake to a bulbous mound.

A mound consumed by wild roots in a green-fingered bind.

At the centre of the mound is a dead, bony white tree.

Its branches have curdled and the blue leaves still clasp on like bats.

She steps onto the peninsula, balancing with her arms out wide –

Foot.

    after…

foot…

    Wobble.

Step.

    by…

step…

Virgil looks down into the lake.

    Through the translucent blue chill of the water is infinity.

    A litany of starlight overwhelmed by a magnificent nebula.

Another great cloud of matter ruptures across the depths

        stretched across the expanding infinite.

        The universe rests at Virgil's feet.

Her eyes are wide, stupefied by the wonders below.
The peninsula widens ahead.
She treads further along.
Always transfixed on the depths.
Virgil leans over the skin of the lake.
Her virgin hair pricks the surface.
Twin galaxies merge and waltz in the depths.
She leans back and looks towards the pale tree on the mound.
The damp tips of her hair drip liquid onyx and stain her robe.
Virgil rises to the mound.

IV
PETRA: MOUND

The dirt mound hangs in a limp stasis.
Water orbits the soil sphere.
Virgil grabs at a root to heave herself up.
Under the bone tree is a kidney shaped pond.
Central to the convex surface is a closed lotus flower.
She feels her way to the pond.
Reaching, touching, yearning to see more.
The pond water is convex, amplifying the depth of the universe.
Barren space - nothing like the wonders held by the lake.
A handful of distant stars twinkle.
She taps the sheath of the water.
A ripple.
The universe enlarges.
A dull red dwarf subsists in dead space.
Its spent, ashen glow is soft over her blank skin.
Virgil touches the water again – the universe shrinks.
She rolls up her sleeve.
Her spectral arm is honeycombed by cerulean veins.
The tip of her finger is wet with a black taint.

Virgil plunges her arm into the swell.

Elbow deep.

She fondles the core of the pond.

And draws her arm out.

A watery GLOOP! and the pond becomes concave.

Now the sights are as magnificent as before.

Another two galaxies merge and oscillate with passion.

Stars dilate, their cores larger and brighter than the last.

A red dwarf mutates into a chunk of raw garnet in the pool.

Virgil takes it out and inspects it.

An air bubble POPS! at the surface.

It tosses a handful of gems onto the mound.

A group of stars have clicked out.

The nebula leaks a sanguine mantis through space.

The galaxies pirouette through the now weeping universe.

One by one supernova reach cataclysm and fade.

Darkening the cosmos in a monochrome wave.

All colour is stolen by the dark menace.

Only red is left.

Virgil looks up from the pond.

The aquamarine lake pulses with a scarlet haze.

The lake is disturbed.

Exquisite jewelled flotsam and jetsam scrape against the mound.

Rubies, emeralds and sapphires regurgitated from the belly of the cosmos.

She drops the garnet back into the pond.

It dissolves into a cloud of amber.

The lake gains an amber glow.

Her face is distorted by the reddening phosphorescence.

She is anxious.

The lake's breaths boom at the shore.

She tosses a sapphire into the pond.

It cools the lake's corona.

Virgil piles all the jewels into the pond.

Her robe is stained black by the lake water.
A multitude of colour slithers over the membrane of the pond.
Virgil's shadows are cast like light through a prism.
                    An apparition in every hue.
                                        Relief.
                Eyelids lap together.
                                            Slow...
        Breaths.
The resonance is gone – the lake is serene.
The lake and the black pond water turn golden and viscous.
Virgil suckles on it.
She washes it over her face, scrubbing at the grime on her plati-
num skin.
Another drink.
                Pink eyes shut.
                                    Breathing slows.
                            Expression blank.
                            She is existing.
Virgil opens one eye to see a fallen leaf frozen in mid fall.
        The lake had taken on an annealed crust.
                                Time had glaciated.
Everything is bound except Virgil,
and the pond.
A sickening tear.
The lotus flower cracks.
Its petals unfurl and exhibit an amber eye.
Blink. Blink.
It rises from the core of the lotus flower on a hairy velveteen
stalk.
Blink. Blink.
The eye stares at Virgil.
Blink. Blink.
It angles forward.
Blink. Blink.

Inquisitive.
Blink. Blink.
Closer.
Blink. Blink.
A pair of ebony mandibles rise from beneath and clamp the stalk.
The eye palpitates.
Amber eyed.
      Tighter.
Suffocating.
      Tighter.
Suffocated.
The obsidian eye separates from the stalk and imprints on the soil.
It pumps with the aggression of a tumor.
      Swells.
             Larger.
A black globular egg waiting to bu-
                 It bursts.
A raven resin discharges.
      Ink in water.
Virgil retches on all fours.
And vomits the black nectar up.
She checks her reflection in the pond.
      A gaunt face.
Cheekbones protrude beneath a yellowed rot.
      Her ivory hair is black at the root.
The ebony cancer is purging her virgin skin.
      The eye is gone.
      The lotus flower still sealed.
    The azure leaf rests upon a root.
The lake exhales once more.
      A cough. A splutter. Vomit.
A clot of tar.
      Another cough. Another splutter. Vomit.

Bile and a twist of the gut.
Virgil crawls towards the dead tree.
And sits against the brittle bough.
Another retch – only bile.
                         Remission from the black.
                              Eyes shut.
                                   Rest.
         That sickening tear.
A marbled hand rises from the pond.
Virgil opens her eyes.
              A faceless humanoid is climbing from the pond.
Its skin is marbled by a plethora of hues.
It stands divine, majestic, pregnant.
The ashen girl pales.
Pantheos,
              Virgil, we are prima.
Finalis.
              Absolute.
                    Pantheos.
Each syllable speckled
by a sharp falsetto,
and an endless baritone.
Pantheos,
              There is nothing Virgil.
You have witnessed unimaginable things,
              the deaths of a million stars,
galaxies that have caroused from beginning to end.
Virgil's pink eyes blacken,
a rasp tugs each breath.
Pantheos,
              Even the end of time.
You hold vigil to the pinnacle of existence.
              You stand whilst the pincer of entropy crumbles
black holes.

The natural state of everything is chaos.
Absolution has no order.
The whites of her eyes are black.
She tears at her hair.
Imploding at the core.
She frantically crawls to the pond.
    The water is black.
      There is no twinkle.
    No ice comets.
      No shooting stars.
   No magnificent nebulae.
Nothing.
Pantheos,
  Offer yourself.
Rebirth.
    Start it all over again.
You've seen many wonders.
   Imagine living everything
     that will ever be.
The birth of a child.
The genius at work.
The death of a tyrant.
    Become the sentinel of collectiveness.
Her black eyes seep two crystal tears.
They carve through stained cheeks.
Pantheos,
  Come.
An open marbled hand.
She takes it.
Pantheos steps into the pond.
She is frozen on the edge.
Pantheos is under the skin of the pond.
    The bone tree cracks.
   A bough slams into the floor.

Tremors from above.

A crack in the sky.

She steps into the pond.

The black water manifests around her.

Cave rocks fall in an almighty schism.

They pound the lake until it exhales no more.

The storm breaks through the cave.

The tar is dissolving Virgil.

Her arms collapse like wet paper.

Her legs give way.

She falls, now only a torso.

Her body is ravaged in a pixelated decay.

AN ALMIGHTY THUNDERCLAP.

Virgil's eyes open wide.

She opens her mouth to wail, but the darkness creeps in.

A gargled moan.

A pronged halcyon bolt strikes the pond.

Then nothing.

CUT TO WHITE.

Rhoda Greaves

Rhoda Greaves is working on a collection of short stories as part of her PhD thesis, after completing an MA in Writing at Birmingham City University. *How the Garden Grows* was first published online at http://www. flash500.com after winning second place in Flash500's flash-fiction writing competition, then published at http://flashfloodjournal.blogspot.co.uk as part of National Flash-Fiction Day.

How the Garden Grows

It was the cord. Wrapped around her like an infant monkey, clinging for life and sparing no thought for Fiona's newborn neck. It sucked out the oxygen and replaced it with a stream of bubbles that scrambled for a foothold in her suckling mind.

As the years go by, Fiona learns that she can think in straight lines if she really concentrates, but mostly her thoughts fight their way to the front like sugary toddlers struggling free from their reins.

She comes to the Centre on weekdays. Meg says it's because her brain didn't grow up. But Fiona knows she's a grown up, as she's ripening a secret – stored away – hidden, especially from Meg.

Her sister Meg picks her up every morning, and drops Fiona at the Centre while she goes to work. Meg is a painter but she doesn't paint walls. Fiona's seen her pictures strung in a big house for everyone to stare at. Meg took her there once, in a posh black frock and treated her to sour lemonade in a tippy-over glass. It made her feel giddy so she'll choose the Coca-Cola if she goes there again.

Fiona doesn't have a mum so Meg looks after her. Meg chooses her clothes and ties back her dead-straight hair in a flowery bandana that Fiona can't fit herself. Meg says it's to stop it hanging limp and making her look special. But Fiona thinks that's silly, as she wants to look special and thinks Meg should want to as well.

When the bandana falls over Fiona's eyes, her keyworker Susie gently removes it, and slides in Fiona's favourite hair clip – the one with the pretty mermaid that makes Fiona sparkle. Susie removes it before Meg returns though, and no one mentions it in case Meg gets cross.

When Fiona asked Meg for a 'Disney Princess' t-shirt, Meg said no, because Fiona's not a child. She got a jumper from Primark. And these brown sandals like Jesus from the Bible. They're too tight now as new blood circles and bites at her toes.

Fiona is a gardener. She grows the flowers that are dried and stuck on Christmas cards – they're sold to raise money for the Centre to buy more seeds.

She doesn't talk much… as when she says things people sometimes stare. But she hums while she crafts – nursery rhymes mostly, that nearly no one hears. She sculpts the soil, patting life into her plants, and places weaklings carefully under plastic bottles to keep them safe from the weather and strangling arms.

Fiona closes her eyes to concentrate and thinks about her secret as she feels it gently flutter. She knows that Meg will see it when she grows as big as a baboon. But now she's quietly cultivating – in nature's plastic bottle. Carefully feeding and watering daily, so her daughter will be blessed with a bubble-free brain.

L. M. Thompson

L.M. Thompson is a video-game obsessed writer and journalist whose fiction has appeared all over the world. In 2012 he was shortlisted for the Eric Hoffer Award for Best New Writer, and in-between writing for *PxlByte* magazine and *Sneaky Bastards* he creates literary fiction often focusing on sociopathic characters. He's not sure why, but he believes that may not be a good sign.

Resolution

Idle eyes on the sweeping swallow flight
Turn gradually downwards,
To salt stains from the sea
And footprints left here amid long
Unsmoked cigarettes,
His path is a rabbit run between
The dead of yesterday and the day before,
And he is the rabbit,
And he is running,
The ache in his side is an armchair
And a winter in whisky,
Often repeated,
The blood forms harsh black borders
Gently contracting,
Letterboxing the stones, the dirt,
The gravel, the dust,
And raising his head,
The horizon, distant and red,
Soughing its shape in a laughter
He swears is directed at him.

Invitation

Tendrils of tallow drip the length of it
Staining, blackly, the rosewood drawer,
As a youth's eye fixes on the quivering
Tip,

Voices are calling,
    Voices from another room,
Familiar,
    Unsteady laughter and the wretched sobs
Of a woman, once known,
They are not voices,
    They are the flame sounds,
The flicker of light on a bedroom wall
Which is a procession of dancing greys,
    The flames are waves,
The waves are singing,

The youth sucks the char from his finger
Licking, wolfishly, the burn on his skin,
As the amber spearing flame fades in the memory
Of his eye.

The Maid

Observing
Through keyhole, corroded brass,
Lips swallowing a cigarette tip
As rag polishes,
Moles on ankles, hairs on arms,
Sharp, unpainted nails,
He nurses his boyhood
In side-piercing shafts
Of sunlight,
Opens his mouth to bite.
    What's that noise?
    What is that noise now?
A trespasser,
Wiping wet hands
On hot thighs.

An Accident

and the rain ceased to fall.

Torches light a shoreline,
A ship, driven to slate,
The incipient arrivals, the hollow words,
    Is there…
    Why isn't…
Boys from town, from hotels,
Crowd together to perform the ritual
Of sucking saliva from rims of pilfered bottles,
Wiping lips on sleeves,
A child hefts a stone yelling for the fun of it all.

Michelle Luka

Michelle Luka has enjoyed writing since childhood, but it took a major accident and the loss of a limb to realise that her lifelong ambitions could no longer be ignored. She made a deal with herself: if she could pass an MA in Writing, then excuses no longer existed, and her story would finally be told.

Snap

Being hit by a speeding car doesn't hurt. But the feeling; I should say numbness, doesn't last long. And then there's the question: is it your brain kicking in to protect you, or a higher force shielding you from the vicious milliseconds of life-changing demolition?

There was an instant of clarity before the car struck. I was like a stag caught in blinding white headlights – then I'm soaring through the air. It's so quiet. Nothing exists in this void of weightlessness. And then it arrives, the sound of a multitude of bones – smashed, snapped, crushed and broken. An image springs to mind here: a colossal glacier just as the big thaw arrives in the arctic springtime.

I had head injuries, broken ribs and a lower body that had just been unplugged from the mains, as well as my very own jigsaw puzzle: a shattered pelvis still missing many pieces today – now held together by rods, screws and pins. I think it's safe to say, Humpty Dumpty has nothing on me.

Each fracture was accompanied by a seismic tremor. That was me, bouncing off the iron railings and flooding the gutter; blocking the drain with a cocktail of dried leaves and syrupy arterial blood: a red berry smoothie – bright, frothy and full of nutrients. I landed, barely conscious, on the January tarmac, as it shimmered with broken glass like frosted diamonds in the night.

What are the chances that a surgeon was walking past that bus stop where I lay, crumpled and oozing a bouquet of crimson, to the shrieking tones of Babylon Zoo's *Space Man*, escaping from the Barton Arms pub? Who was she? I'll never know, nobody ever did, though if ever there was a right place at the right time – that was it.

Before that night I'd received five messages. You could say they were warnings: information about my future. There was a strange encounter with an enigmatic elderly lady who turned up in the dental surgery, where I worked, one lunch break. Then there were the disturbing and accurate tarot readings by my friend, Clint. Stranger still, were the vivid dreams my mum and I shared the night before the accident: I had been watching my own funeral on a sandy beach as the tide came in. Mum had dreamt that a woman had taken me out of her arms as a baby, before placing another child into her embrace, telling her that this was her new little girl and she was to love and care for her as much as the last.

Two days before the accident, in the block of flats where I lived, I could see a distinct image of a goblin hovering in the right corner of the lift. It could have been a trick of the mind, I suppose, but I was completely sober and drug free. I put it down to tiredness.

On the actual morning I received junk mail; health insurance mainly. Throwing the contents into the bin, out fell a hard plastic card with my name in black letters, and beneath this the words: *In Case of Emergency,* then in red ink on the next line down – Rhesus B positive: my blood group.

The Tarot Reading

It was the second week of January and Clint decided he'd read my tarot. It was a bit of fun: I wanted to know whether love was on the cards for the forthcoming year. We'd dabbled a few times but nothing major, not on my part. I was always a little apprehensive but Clint, who was and still is extremely spiritual, held great respect for these objects. He assured me that nothing evil could ever come of them, they simply create balance to the ebb and flow of your life. I still believe this to be true.

I opted to draw random cards from the pack. We used 'Major Arcana' tarot cards. Of all the cards, these are the most spiritual deck and are said to carry deep meaning. There was no limit to the number of cards I could select. Clint said to stop when I felt it was right: I stopped at seven.

It came as no surprise that the first card I drew was *The Fool*. I took offence. The image was of a Jester carrying a bag on his back, off on his merry travels, blissfully unaware of the threatening tidal wave creeping up behind him.

'Do I look like an arse to you?' I'd said.

Clint leant back on his elbows opposite to where I lounged on the floor facing him, the deck placed ominously on the grey carpet between us.

'It isn't saying that at all.' He explained that I was about to begin a new life that was going to take me on an important journey; this could be physical, mental or spiritual. There would be changes. The loss of naivety, innocence and impulsiveness – things I very much possessed at that time.

'You're about to grow up; it's time to stand on your own two feet,' he announced. I was disappointed.

The second card zapped my mouth of saliva: *The Tower*. It was on fire with two people tumbling out to their death. Forks of lightening and all manner of national geographic catastrophes: giant hailstones, fire and brimstone plunging the fairy-tale tower into a monstrous raging sea. All I wanted to know was whether I was going to find love and romance that year. Not a big ask. 'No lovely happy ending for me then?'

'Get over yourself! Who's going to want to shag a desperate hag like you?' Clint ducked his head just in time to dodge the cushion. 'Oh, but look at this!' He clutched the card high above his head and began to read out loud. Everything I knew: my life, routines, comfort, job, health; all of it was about to fall to pieces. A path of mayhem appeared on the horizon: disruption, conflict and chaos. Did I mention upheaval – widespread and cataclysmic repercussions?

'But don't worry,' Clint added, 'it also means a happy ending: enlightenment and freedom.' You could hear the drip from the tap in the kitchen, the silence between us was that... silent.

When my eyes fastened on the third card: *The Hanged Man*, a grain of anxiety morphed into a rock in the pit of my stomach. There was a man hanging upside down on a wooden T-shaped branch. He had his left leg tucked up high beneath his right, giving the impression that the lower half of his limb was missing.

Clint could see the tension on my face. 'Don't get yourself all worked up you crazy cow!' This card meant limbo: a time of transition, a period of waiting and sacrifice. He described it as the process a caterpillar goes through in order to become a butterfly. It was going to be a long and arduous task.

'It could be your job. You keep going on about wanting to become a dental hygienist – it might be about all the studying and money involved. You won't be able to go out on the piss all the time anymore; that's your sacrifice. And then you'll emerge the other end all qualified and up your own arse. I'm telling you, that's what it is.'

I didn't believe him. It had taken me three attempts to pass my dental nursing qualification. No way was becoming a hygienist on the cards. There was no sign of love either, only problems and uncertainties. And then the card came along that dragged my guts ten feet under.

I snatched the cigarette from Clint's mouth. Despite being asthmatic, I took a long drag and proceeded to choke. Clint lit another for himself. The letters were large and uncanny: they scorched my eyeballs as the word *Death* filled my vision.

'It's not what you think,' he sighed, clearly fed up of my dramatics.

'Oh piss off!' This was a new year, and I wanted to begin it with optimism, but instead I'd drawn a pile of shit cards, this one, the most shit of them all.

I could not tear my eyes from the skeleton in the black suit of armour sitting upon a noble white horse. The knight's helmet was open, revealing his skull with vacant black orbs where his eyes should have been. His bony metacarpals clutched a black banner with a large white crest and roman numerals that were too small to decipher. Two young children were knelt at his feet, their gaze cast away from his shrouded presence. Beneath the horse lay a dead man in elegant robes. And a gentleman of greater refinement dressed in rich attire, stood worshipping this dark spectre.

Clint chuckled like the *Grinch*, 'This is not a card foretelling your death, far from it.' He relished the rollercoaster of emotions he'd inflicted upon me. Death meant the opposite of the word, he explained. The beginning of a new life after having gone through major life-altering circumstances: a permanent end to a previous existence, much like the aforementioned caterpillar and butterfly. It signified transformation, a new way of life. *Auld Lang Syne* echoed in my ear.

He hadn't eased my mind one bit. There were too many changes upon the horizon. Where was the love? Why couldn't I have love? It hadn't been mentioned once and I was determined, more out of principle than anything else. I continued to draw cards.

The Chariot only added to this surreal reading. A man of wealth and stature stood in his chariot. Sitting at either side of him were a pair of Egyptian sphinx or lions, it was hard to tell which. Off into the distance lay a city. 'Haven't a clue,' I sighed.

'This is a good one.' Clint became animated, his green eyes wide with excitement. This was victory, the end of a long period of turmoil and suffering, overcoming life's biggest obstacles using a wealth of perseverance and determination. This card meant prevailing where others have failed: acceptance in one's circumstances, a great will to continue onwards and upwards.

It was small relief to know that what I was to go through wouldn't be permanent, but the cards did seem to be changing for the better. When I saw the next one, I couldn't have been more eager for the reading.

I had selected *The Lovers*, but of course, this wasn't about finding love. I was looking at an image of Adam and Eve in the Garden of Eden. Eve stood on the left beside the apple tree where a giant snake entwined itself. Adam was on her right next to a taller tree. In the distance were mountains and above their heads, pink candyfloss clouds where an enormous golden-haired angel with wings spread wide, hovered beneath a vast blazing sun.

Once again, this card represented the opposite of all my hopes and dreams: contradiction, deception, disharmony, duality and a struggle within. Distrust in partnerships, the inability to stay in a monogamous relationship: infidelity, disloyalty and a hardening of the heart. Whatever was about to happen in my life: that date, April 4th 2003 was the catalyst.

The Wheel of Fortune, was the final card in the sequence, and in contrast it oozed wellbeing and happiness.

'Joy of joys!' Clint sang out, sitting up and crossing his legs underneath him. This card meant good luck, positive change, letting go of past events and moving on to better times. Here was good fortune and advancement. The start of another new cycle bringing in new beginnings: a life of karma, enlightenment, destiny, spirituality, knowledge, reward, fulfilment, luck and success: and above all, everlasting love.

'So, in order for me to get peace, love and all the good stuff, I have to go through torment, suffering, pain and... hell?' I asked him.

Clint looked down, studying the seven tiny soothsayers laid out before him, then lifted his eyes to meet mine. 'Well, according to the cards, I'd say... yes.'

Sheryl Browne

Sheryl Browne is a partner in business, a mother, and a foster parent to disabled dogs. Creative in spirit, Sheryl has always had a passion for writing and is now thrilled to be published by Safkhet Publishing. Keen to improve her writing, Sheryl is studying for an MA in Creative Writing at Birmingham City University.

The Memory Box

Damn. Daniel Adams cursed silently, noting the thunderous look on his son's face. There was a time and a place for carefree frivolity, and their lounge – with a whole other family, when Jake had lost such a huge part of his – wasn't it.

Raking a hand through his hair, Daniel walked over to him. 'Hey, Jake, how's it going? We were just… ' He stopped, searching for a way to explain. Andrea and her family were only there until their own house was habitable, but still, it must seem to Jake as if she was trying to replace his mother.

'Sorting through the clothes people have kindly donated,' Andrea supplied, 'before Ryan's forced to go out chatting up babes in his boxers.'

Jake's expression didn't alter. He glanced at Andrea, then dragged his eyes back to Daniel.

Daniel placed a hand on his shoulder. 'You *are* going to get some breakfast, Jake, before you and Ryan go –'

Jake pulled away. 'Not hungry.'

Right. Daniel blew out a breath. 'Jake, you either eat something, or you don't get to go into town today. Your choice.'

'Whatever.' Jake turned to walk towards the stairs, shrugging scrawny shoulders under his rugby shirt as he went.

'Jake!' Daniel called after him.

'What?' Jake didn't turn back.

'The kitchen's that way. Get some breakfast, please,' Daniel said calmly, though his patience was wearing thin. How in hell was he going to get Jake to talk to him, if they couldn't even communicate on a rudimentary level?

Jake did turn around then. 'Why?' he asked, his eyes holding a defiant challenge.

'Because I said so, Jake.'

'And what gives *you* the right to tell *me* what to do?' Jake demanded, his expression now bordering on hatred.

So here it was. Standoff time. Jake's fury about to be unleashed and he had no clue how to respond. 'I'm your dad, Jake,' he tried, sounding feeble, even to his own ears. 'If I ask you to do something, it's because I –'

'Care?' Jake gauged him through narrowed his eyes. 'Yeah, right.' He sneered, and turned away.

'Jake… ' Daniel counted silently to five. 'You either do as I say and eat something, or you're grounded.'

'Yeah, yeah.' Jake walked on up the stairs. '*Yadda yadda yadda.*'

'I mean it, Jake.'

'Whatever.'

Daniel tried very hard to remain calm. 'Jake, come back down, please.'

Jake stopped on the stairs, breathing hard, his shoulders tense. 'No,' he said shortly.

'Now, Jake!'

Jake whirled around. 'No!' He swiped a hot, angry tear from his face. 'I'm not doing *anything* you say! Why should I?' he shouted. Christ, how Daniel wished he could close the gap, climb the stairs, hold him. Tell the kid to hit him, kick him, whatever it took to make him feel better.

'Jake, come on…' He took a tentative step towards him.

'Get stuffed!' Jake stopped him in his tracks. 'You don't care about me. You don't care about anybody. You didn't even care about Mum!'

Christ. Daniel felt the blood drain from his face. He couldn't do this. He swallowed hard. Not here. Not now. In front of… He glanced back at Andrea, his own breathing heavy. 'I… ' he started, shook his head and took another step forwards. 'Jake…'

'No!' Jake yelled. 'You *never* cared about her. You never did *that* with her.' He nodded towards the lounge. 'Mum never laughed after she was ill when *you* were around. Never!' Jake's expression told Daniel all he needed to know. Jake did hate him, with every bone in his body. He'd every right to. And it hurt more than anything had ever done in his life.

'Let me try,' Andrea suggested gently, as Jake turned on his heel and flew up the stairs.

Daniel looked at her bewildered, incapable of coordinating his thoughts let alone his speech.

'We have a bereavement plan in place at the school,' Andrea explained. 'To help children like Jake cope. He might let me talk to him. You never know.'

* * *

'He's good in a crisis,' Andrea went on talking to herself, as she had been the last five minutes. Still Jake refused to acknowledge her, his expression stony, his eyes fixed to his PC.

'He has to use a sat-nav to find the kitchen, but he makes a mean Pepsi Max,' she went on, expounding her son's dubious culinary skills.

Still no response.

'A cup of tea is beyond him, unfortunately, which Ryan's always at pains to point out,' Andrea chatted on, 'he being a man and therefore incapable of multitasking, he says, i.e. putting teabags in the cups whilst boiling the kettle.'

Silence was Jake's answer.

'Of course, this is after he's hilariously balanced the kettle on his head, because I've made the fatal mistake of asking him to put it *on*.' Andrea waited, wondering what on earth she could say that might at least elicit some response, however small.

Jake shrugged again, then... *Yes*! There it was, a definite upward twitch to his mouth. 'I'll go and see if he's managed to negotiate his way to your kitchen yet, shall I, before we dehydrate up here?'

Jake nodded. Definitely progress, Andrea thought, heading for the door. Pepsi Max and chocolate biscuits were probably not the most balanced breakfast, but at least Jake might eat something if she and Ryan joined him.

'He doesn't talk about her,' Jake blurted, behind her.

Andrea turned back. 'Do you want him to, Jake?'

Jake dragged his forearm hurriedly across his eyes. 'Uh-huh.' He nodded, trying hard to force back his tears. 'He never says anything. It's like he's scared or something. Like the kids at school, where I went before. No one ever asked me about Mum after she died. No one ever said anything. They just looked, and whispered stuff to each other.'

Andrea sat back down next to him, as close as she dared without invading his space. 'Why was that Jake, do you think?'

Another shrug.

'Because they thought it might make you sad, possibly?'

'Maybe,' Jake conceded. 'The thing is...' he hesitated '... it does make me sad sometimes, really sad. But I *want* to talk about her. She was my mum.' He glanced at Andrea as if he couldn't quite understand why people didn't get it.

'I'm sure your mum knew you loved her, Jake. Mums do, you know? It's instinctive. We feel it in here.' Andrea placed a hand over her heart.

Jake's eyes slid towards her again. 'She said she was scared. Scared for him.'

'Your dad?' Andrea probed softly.

Jake nodded. 'She said she was scared for me, too, but that she knew I knew she'd always love me and watch out for me. She didn't think he... knew she loved him, though.'

Andrea took a breath, her heart breaking for this little boy and his lost father. 'Adults don't see things so clearly sometimes, Jake.' She saw a chance and took his hand. He didn't pull away.

'Sometimes emotions get in the way. Do you understand?'

Jake nodded again. 'Like anger?'

'Yes, anger. Hurt, sadness. Sometimes they stop you saying what you really feel.'

'I did tell her I loved her,' Jake confided, after a second. 'When she was ill, she tried really hard, you know?' He turned at last to look directly at Andrea, his eyes full to brimming. 'To make sure I was all right. Make me smile and stuff. She tried to make sure things would be okay for me and... Dad too, making lists of where things were and how stuff worked. I was kind of proud of her, you know?'

Andrea did know, absolutely. The sense of the woman she'd felt whilst looking through her things. Even knowing how ill she was, Michelle Adams had been strong for her family, yet as gentle and caring as a mother could be.

'You know something, Jake,' she said, feeling humbled. 'There isn't a mum anywhere who wouldn't be proud of a son who could say out loud that he loved her.'

Jake pulled in a breath, his skinny chest puffing up. 'I'd like to tell people more about her, but...'

'No one gives you chance?'

'It's like everyone's pretending she never existed,' Jake said quietly.

'How about we make a memory box, Jake?' Andrea suggested, knowing that he needed to dwell, but on the good things.

Jake squinted at her curiously.

'We'll make up a box of special things you can remember her by. Photographs, and such like.'

Jake thought about it, then nodded. 'They're in the spare room,' he said, scrambling off the bed as Ryan came in with a tray laden with biscuits, essential sugar-high fizzy stuff and an actual cup of tea.

'And anything else you can think of, Jake,' Andrea said. 'Things that will help you to think about the good times.'

'Her perfume. I've got some in my room. It makes me remember her better.' Jake made a grab for his Pepsi. 'And Harry Potter,' he added, wiping his mouth on his shirtsleeve as he headed on out.

'I'll give you a hand, mate,' Ryan offered, giving Andrea a knowing wink as he plonked the tray down. 'Not sure Harry Potter will fit in the box,' he said, heading after Jake, 'but...'

'Dimwit. I meant the book.' Jake's child-bordering-on-adolescent tones drifted back. 'Mum used to read it to me at bedtime.'

'Cool. Which one?'

'*Goblet of Fire. Prisoner of Azkaban.* Most of them, until she died. Have you read them?'

'Yep. Got them all,' Ryan said, cranking up his enthusiasm for Jake's sake. Bless his mismatched *Simpsons* socks. 'Or I did have, before the fire.'

'Aw, that sucks,' Jake said. 'You could share mine.'

'Cool,' Ryan said, with rather less enthusiasm.

* * *

'Jake?' Daniel knocked on his son's door.

Would he answer this time? Probably not.

Daniel reached for the handle, only to find the door opened by Ryan.

'Hi. How's it going?' Daniel smiled at the gangly teenager, who, far from being the bad influence Daniel had worried he might be, seemed to be sprouting a halo along with some stubble – and who Daniel reckoned deserved a medal for looking out for Jake.

'Yeah, good. Just helping Jake sort some stuff out.'

'Oh?' Daniel glanced past Ryan into the room, to where Jake sat cross-legged on the floor, no PlayStation control in sight, amazingly. 'What stuff would that be then, Jake?'

Daniel waited, but took his cue when Ryan motioned him in.

'Off to get some more Pepsi, mate,' Ryan said diplomatically. 'Want some?'

Jake nodded, but didn't look up.

'Back in ten.' Ryan drooped out, skinny fit jeans still clinging to hips, looking every inch the typical allergic-to-anything-strenuous teenager. Daniel owed the kid, that was for sure.

He owed Jake too, big time.

Daniel turned his attention back to his son, who was surrounded by a sea of photographs. Photographs of Michelle, from the albums in the spare room.

Cautiously, Daniel walked across to stand by Jake's side. Then, hands in pockets, he waited again, wondering what to say that could even begin to heal their relationship. What would *he* want to hear, if he were Jake?

Sorry perhaps? Wholly inadequate, Daniel knew, but it might be a start.

He looked down at his son, whose head was bent in concentration. He needed a haircut. Needed a lot of things. Daniel closed his eyes, as he noticed the bottle of perfume tucked in the corner of Jake's Adidas shoebox.

'Need any help, Jake?' Daniel asked softly.

Jake didn't answer. That was okay. Daniel didn't really expect him to. He swallowed back a lump in his throat, then took a gamble, crouched down next to Jake – and silently prayed.

Biding his time, he studied the photographs alongside his son. 'You've chosen all the good ones,' he ventured.

Jake did respond then, somewhere between a nod and a shrug.

'Not many fun ones though.' Daniel reached for a photograph. One he'd taken himself on what had turned out to be their last time at the theme park together: Michelle – Jake in front of her on the log flume, both shrieking with laugher and soaked through to the skin. Probably the last time she had laughed – with him.

Daniel breathed in, hard. 'I did make her sad Jake,' he said quietly. 'I'm sorry. I know it doesn't help much, but... I wish to God I hadn't.'

Jake's head dropped even lower.

'She did laugh though, you know, Jake,' Daniel pushed on, 'with you.'

He placed the photograph carefully in the box. 'Alton Towers,' he said, 'summer before last. She laughed so much she had to dash to the loo, remember?'

Jake dragged the back of his hand under his nose.

'She couldn't have been that happy without you, Jake. You gave her the gift of laughter. That's something to be glad about. To be proud of.'

Daniel stopped, his chest filling up as he watched a slow tear fall from his son's face. Daniel hesitated, then rested a hand lightly on Jake's shoulder.

Jake didn't shrug him off.

'You won her a stuffed toy that day, do you remember? What was it? A tiger?'

'Tigger.' Jake finally spoke.

'That's right,' Daniel said, his throat tight. 'Tigger.'

'She kept it in the car,' Jake picked up in a small voice.

The car she never arrived at the hospital in. 'She kept a whole family of furry friends in the car,' he said. 'I'm surprised there was room for her.'

Jake's mouth twitched into a small smile. 'She talked to them.' He glanced up at Daniel, his huge blue eyes glassy with tears.

'That was the little girl inside her. The little girl you made laugh.' Daniel squeezed Jake's shoulder.

He actually felt like whooping. Like punching the air. Like picking Jake up and hugging him so hard... He'd *looked* at him. Full on. No anger.

Daniel closed his eyes, relief washing over him. 'I have one of Mum's stuffed toys,' he said throatily. 'One she kept. Not Tigger, but... Do you want me to fetch it?'

Jake nodded.

'Right.' Daniel smiled. 'Back in two,' he dragged his forearm across his eyes as he headed for his own room. He had something else, too. Something he'd wanted to give Jake before, but somehow couldn't.

The antique locket he'd bought Michelle for her thirtieth was in the bedside drawer. Daniel ran his thumb over the engraved rose-gold surface of it. If Jake needed something to remind him of his mother...

'Bedtime Bear,' Daniel announced, joining Jake back on the floor. 'Your very first toy.' He handed the scruffy little white bear to his son.

Jake laughed – and Daniel really did feel like crying.

'I have something else for you, Jake.' He passed him the locket. 'It was very special to her,' he said gently, as Jake's eyes fell on the photograph of himself inside it. 'She wore it right next to her heart. And that,' he went on as Jake looked at the lock of hair on the opposite side of the locket, 'is your hair and hers, entwined.'

Jake went very quiet.

'Okay?' Daniel asked.

Jake nodded vigorously. 'Okay,' he said, around a sharp intake of breath.

Daniel reached out, ran his hand through Jake's unruly crop, and then allowed it to stray to his shoulder. He wanted very much to hold him, to reassure him. But Jake's body language was tense. It would take time, Daniel knew, but maybe, someday, Jake would let him back in.

Emma Taylor

Emma Taylor is aged twenty and in her second year at Birmingham City University, studying English and Creative Writing. She lives at home in Coventry. *Hourglass* was written in a creative writing seminar after a class discussion about flash fiction.

Hourglass

The hourglass turns and the grains fall. Every event has the potential to be as grand as a musical movement: some sharp, others flat. Some major, others minor. The grains fall and diminish. There could be years left – months – or maybe even days.

John and Mary hadn't spent a lifetime together, nor had they passed through many movements, but their devotion to each other could last a lifetime.

As her last grain dropped, he squeezed her hand.

Jay Boodhoo

Born in Mauritius, Jay Boodhoo came to England in 1972 aged 19 to pursue a career in nursing and nurse education. After four decades working in the NHS and Higher Education, he decided to become a student again at the tender age of 60. He plans to travel, cook, garden and spend quality time with his grandson Asher Jude, in the hope that these will inspire him to write... creatively, of course.

Gods and Dreams

Devika was woken up in the middle of the night by an unbearable pain in her stomach. She feared the worst this time. She somehow knew it was to be an end to her quest. The spare bedroom had become her refuge for the past few weeks, not wishing to get in the way of anyone. That was her nature. She could deal with her hurt without the patronising sympathy she had got used to recently. Five years of hope and disappointment had armoured her spirit, and now she felt she was starting to stand up for herself. She had nothing to lose in whatever decision she would make. She felt emboldened, yet at the same time a wave of vulnerability pulsed in her blood now and then. She was waiting for battle to begin. The moment was approaching and she lay on the makeshift bed on her side curled up in a foetal position. She stared at the unpainted walls and then at her red wedding sari, which hung clumsily as an improvised curtain against the only window in the room. The panes had not been fixed yet, but four vertical bars were secured to the wall to prevent any intruders. She felt secure here but she thought of herself as a prisoner in her own jail.

The room was bare of furniture except for a mirror, which she used every morning to apply her make up before she left for work. Her Chanel lipsticks lay in a neat row on the floor, standing to attention like soldiers, ready to come to her rescue should she need help. The girl in the department store convincingly suggested these would be perfect for her – complementing her light, soft skin and silky black hair perfectly. She loved the vibrant colour, and did not mind spending money on quality. Surrounding these soldiers was all her make up paraphernalia, neatly laid out. She felt weak from the day's fasting in readiness for the full moon tonight. Through the red sari, the full moon had assumed a very bright red glow as if it was about to burst into a blazing inferno. A gentle wind blew through the window and cooled the room. The end of her sari fluttered like a flag at half-mast. She felt no emotional attachment to it nor guilt about its new function. A red hue filled the room as she started to think about the past.

She tried to deflect her pain by turning her thoughts to the half-completed house. How could they have run out of money? What happened to her half of her monthly salary that she was putting away into the building pot? Should she have taken over the overseeing of the building project?

'Of course not. I am always reminded that I am a woman,' she thought out aloud. She would not have been trusted with such 'manly tasks.'

With her head for numeracy and planning, she would have been perfect for the overseeing of the building project. She could not understand how a shortfall could occur. They had done all the calculations together and had factored in her treatment. There was a clash of priorities. Completing the house building? Continuing with her programme? There were accusations, followed by arguments. Then came the blame placing and the long silences. And, for her, it was the retreat in denials.

As she started to drift into a daze, a sudden jolt made her curl into a ball. She felt a sharp knife had come alive inside her and was cutting. The unbearable pain made her faint. She tried to control this by deep breathing, but was gasping out for air. Screaming would have eased her pain but she bit her lips, not wanting to disturb the neighbourhood through her open window. She staggered out of bed and propped her right shoulder against the wall to steady herself. She guided her small frame and her reluctant feet over what felt like a wobbly floor and snail paced to the shrine room. She stopped momentarily by the main bedroom door to pause for breath. Her right ear flattened against the door and her brain filled with the sounds of an angry chainsaw, which, like a lit fuse, set her pain further ablaze. The cramps were shooting towards her back. She wanted to scream to draw attention. There was no point. Her face was contorted and her skin had assumed a bright red colour and, just like the full moon earlier, her head wanted to explode. With both hands she tightly squeezed her lower abdomen as if to prise out an elusive monster that had somehow got inside her. She was bent double. Another disaster? Another loss? Another loss of face? How many more times? She started to sob.

It felt a lifetime before she came face-to-face with her God in the shrine room. She had to fight her way in the small room, as someone had used her holy room as a store cupboard. Dodging the half-used tins of paints, some of them left open with the brushes resting on top of the tins, she managed to negotiate through the rubble. Cut pieces of wood were pushed against the walls. A bag of cement was propped up next to Hanuman, the Monkey God. Saws and hammers were secured behind as if they were his props. This room was her pride and joy and she was alarmed that the ugly debris amidst the serenity of her beloved deity would anger him. An intoxicating mix of paint fumes and incense sent her into a stuporous trance and momentarily dulled her senses. The thought of her holy space being transgressed and desecrated hurt her more than the pain.

Hanuman, in a bright and splendid vermilion, holding a mountain in one hand above his shoulder and a mace in the other, stood looking ahead unconcerned at the carnage around him. Devika joined her hands, wept, and said softly, 'what do I do?' She lay prostrate on the floor in front of Hanuman. It was Devika's choice to have this shrine dedicated to Him as the symbol of strength, perseverance and devotion – qualities she'd aspired to, ever since her mother started taking her to the local temple following the death of her father. On the wall above the statue of Hanuman hung a framed picture of Parvati, goddess symbolizing fertility, marital fidelity and devotion to the spouse. The two in tandem would, she thought, be her fail-safe plan. Her insurance policy.

With great difficulty, she tucked her legs under her into the lotus position, to see if some yoga might override the raw pain. It was always her default mode. She had found this comforting before when she had been through trying times. As she closed her eyes, she heard something giving way. Parvati was sliding down the wall in slow motion. It was a long time before she could hear the shattering of glass. The symbol of fertility seemed to have had enough. Devika felt the sharp knife break in her stomach. The pain ceased and left her body abruptly. She should have felt the joy of release. Her earlier burning pain gave way to a surge of scorching rage.

She stared at Hanuman and let out a pent up, frenzied scream. 'Why? Why now?'

Plumes of smoke from the incense sticks danced in front of Hanuman's face, giving the impression that he was shaking his head. Was he saying yes or no? Was he angry at being screamed at? She half expected the bedroom door to open and someone to wrap their consoling arms round her. Hanuman stared in the distance as if it was none of his business, while Parvati lay under the thousand pieces of cracked glass The angry chainsaw changed its tune to the hoarse croaking, a noise that had become so familiar over the years. Sometimes tolerable, at most times insufferable. She felt so lonely. How could she feel that way? Hanuman was looking on, Parvati was on the floor, and the angry chainsaw was nearby. Yet she felt emptiness in her being. The Gods had left her bereft. Her insurance policy was void.

Devika's prayers had come to nothing. She felt a sense of helplessness. At stake were her own expectations, and the expectations of her Hindu culture. But the expectations of a critical mother-in-law loomed large in her mind. Had failure got a price? Yes, she thought. The price of stigma and ostracisation. With all these thoughts in her head, she surveyed the marks of bloodshot fingerprints where she had tenaciously grabbed her delicate pale skin. They resembled the injury of a fighter engaged in a bare-knuckle fight. She was uncertain if her fight had ended. Or was it just the beginning?

She tried to level with the Gods. Having been in this room so many times, she felt she could talk to Him one-to-one, just like talking to a friend. It was a familiarity that unnerved her, but she needed to salvage something.

'OK Lord Hanuman. I have no quarrels with you. But I need strength to deal with others. Will you help me with that? It is not much to ask, is it? This is the least you can do, given that I have been here every morning. I invested a lot of me in you. Give me your answer and I will go and do whatever I have to do.'

Devika thought she was asking too many questions of her God. Was she pleading too much? She surprised herself. She had never talked to a God like that. She started to feel some logical thoughts connecting in her head.

'If I can talk to Hanuman like this, then why not with others.'

She started to feel a little bolder. She searched for a key under the rubble, shuffled outside the shrine room and locked the door, leaving Lord Hanuman bemused and Parvati still lying desperately on the floor. She left her Gods. This room had never been locked in five years.

Punch-drunk with tiredness she staggered to her bed. The main bedroom door had no intention of opening up. It let its sleeper engage in a deep slumber, untouched by events in the house. Devika fell onto the bed and muttered, 'Please no more dreams tonight.'

She feared that her dreams would end up shattered and splintered, just like the glass in the shrine room. Soon, she was in a deep slumber.

The front door opens of its own accord. There is neither the sound of a key nor the knob turning. As it opens to its widest, a blinding bright light floods the entrance. A figure appears. She can make out an outline of a little boy standing. She feels warmth surging through her body. She feels good. She squints into the brightness to catch a good glimpse. He looks familiar. The gait. The outline of his face. The haircut, fringed at the front. The small thin body. A familiar silhouette in her life and dreams, who comes uninvited but she always welcomes him. A regular visitor who floats in the deep recesses of her mind as if he has claimed the inside of her head as his own territory. She calls out but the sounds remain stuck in her throat. She beckons the boy towards her to hold him. Her arms are too heavy. She attempts to move towards the child. Her feet are cemented to the floor. The child recognises her.

'Where have you been, Ma? I have been waiting a long time. Please hold me.'

And just as he appears, he vanishes instantly leaving her grief stricken and guilty...

Our Shining Light

Just a little something about an event in our life over 30 years ago.
Showed it to my wife last night and we shed a few tears. I would like
to share it with you.

They said that sunlight would eclipse you,
That the moon's smile will never caress you,
That our arms would not hug you in embrace.

But you held tightly inside so secure,
The rope mooring you warm and safe.
Our touches made you float in delight
And your tiny tender fingers waved.

Then you stepped out.
Eyes tightly shut.
Mouth ajar.
Wanting to say something.
I planted a goodbye on your forehead.
You seemed to smile,
You did not see our drowned eyes,
You did not hear our aching sobs.

Then you said goodnight
And joined the stars.
We look for you every day.
Sometimes you twinkle bright
In the vastness of sky,
Your glow
Reminding us that you
Are still our shining light.

Hayley Harman

Hayley Harman is currently studying English Literature and Creative Writing at Birmingham City University. She loves dogs, the colour blue and is Jasmine Laurel Kumar's No.1 fan.

My Mate

It's a busy day. Jam packed. Some say, 'And one for yourself, darlin'.' So I have them. It's the only day of the year we can drink behind the bar. It's Carly's uncle's bar. She got me the job. He gives me a tenner for my taxi from the till. I guess that's my bonus. Carly's got the day off. She'd shown her face for a bit earlier on. I don't mind working today though. It beats moping around at my flat. I hear, 'Don't be late tomorrow,' as I head for the door.

I don't have long to get ready before I head over to Carly's. When I get there I walk straight in, shout, 'Hello,' and head to the kitchen. There's loads of booze on the side. I help myself to a vodka and lemonade and lean against the cooker. I hear Carly coming through shouting, 'Merry Christmas.' We give each other a hug. She looks really good, as always. She says, 'Your hair looks pretty.' 'Thanks,' I say and have a swig. I haven't done much to my hair, just tied it up. 'I like your shoes,' I say, looking at her feet. They're a present from her mum and dad, and her dress. I tell her I got mine from Littlewoods. I had to pay extra to have it delivered the day before, in time for the party. I say her dress is lovely and she smiles, says thanks and asks if I want a top up. I do, so I neck my glass and hand it to her. She knows what I'm having.

We head into the living room. There's some old-school Christmas CD on but I can still hear the fire spitting. Her mum's tree takes pride of place in the window, the little lights playing kiss chase all over it. Her mum and dad are nestled in the sofa sipping Bailey's while Nan sits on a kitchen chair by the window. She's got her stick beside her. I've never seen her without it. We all do the cheek kissing and that, the usual, and I plop myself down next to Carly's mum and we chat away. She asks if I've had a good day. I tell her I didn't leave till five. We'd shut at four but there were a lot of glasses to clear up. 'It was packed when we popped in,' she says. I tell her it was like that till close but I'd got a few tips and some drinks. She shows me her new bracelet and I point out my new dress. They've given Carly some money to put down on a car and I say how lucky she is. We talk about other Christmassy stuff and get on to the turkey. I can see the rest of it set out on a table with batches, pickles, mince pies and that. We laugh about turkey curry, turkey and ham pie, turkey and custard. Carly takes my glass and fills it again. I'm really getting into it; I think turkey flapjacks get in there at one point, and then Carly says her brother and John are on their way. My cheeks light up like cigarette ends.

They're a year older than us. But we hang around together sometimes. We'll go out, or stay in, drink, sometimes smoke, watch films, play music, slag 'the city' off, slag other people off, slag everything off, and laugh. This one time, her brother went to Magaluf with this bird he was seeing. We got holiday envy so went camping for the weekend at a water park. We got really pissed and John said that Carly was like his little sister. She made a big fuss about it: going on that they weren't related. It was funny. That's the sort of stuff we get up to. And I like John. I mean, like, like.

I hear them get out a cab. They sing *Jingle Bells* and laugh all the way through the front door. They're loud. They come into the living room draped across each other shouting, 'Merry Christmas!' There's more kisses and hugs all round, more talk of dinner and then the oldies settle down to talk of relatives no longer here and that. Fuck that. We head to the kitchen. They chat about being at the pub last night. Carly was working and the other two came in after their last shift till after Christmas. I had the night off but had to wash my clothes and stuff as I've only got New Year's Day off so I missed it all. Carly starts on about this pissed up girl hanging all over John. I see Carly smirk but they're all laughing so I join in. John goes, 'Imagine putting up with that from your missis,' and they laugh some more. We have a shot of Sambuca each then Carly fixes us some more drinks.

I go and stand by the food table and John comes over. He asks if I've had a good day. I tell him about work and my tips and how busy I've been. He says he never goes the pub Christmas day. Always stays at home. It's like a family tradition. Carly brings our drinks in. John says she looks lovely, as always. She smiles and flicks her hair. Then John goes, 'But look at you, don't you scrub up well?' I say thanks and look at my glass. Carly says, 'Are you going to drink that or just stare at it?' She seems mad about something. I just shrug and slurp away but I swear I can hardly taste the lemonade in this one. John asks us how work's going. We both say it's ok. I say I'm thinking of going to college in the new year. He goes to ask about it but Carly tells him she's getting a car. So they start talking about what kind of car she's getting and stuff like that instead.

I go over to Carly's brother and chat to him for a while. He turns the music up a touch and it starts to feel like a party. Next thing, some of the neighbours knock the door. They come in with a bottle of something. We all have a shot – Whiskey or something – and even though I don't know them that well I'm giving them Christmas kisses too. Christmas does that. People just forget shit and have a good time. Then Carly's nan decides she needs to pee and there's this mission to get her up the stairs. She makes it across the front room by herself, using that stick. I follow behind the group. There's one on the stairs in front and one behind her, kind of heaving her up, and two people standing there telling the ones on the stairs to do what they're already doing anyway. I laugh. I go to the kitchen but it's empty so I spin around and walk back out again and see she's only one more step up. I lick the sticky stuff off my hand and check to see if there's a hole in my glass. Then I say, 'Why don't you just get her the mop bucket?' I get a look from Carly's mum.

Back in the front room I tell them what I've said and we have a laugh. There's a bit of dancing going on now and voices are getting louder. Carly's two cousins arrive next. They're nice girls. I know them from the pub. So we're all dancing away when Carly decides I need another drink. I say, 'I've got work tomorrow,' but she insists. 'It's Christmas,' she says, 'let your hair down.' I say, 'Ok,' and take my hairband out. We both laugh. She brings me another drink. I see she still has her old one. I go, 'Where's yours?' and she says she'll have one in a minute. I say, 'Oh,' and have a gulp of mine. There's a real noise in the place now. I think I should eat something so I head to the table. Others have been nibbling away. I get a paper plate and put a few bits on and munch in. John comes over and gets something too. He asks what I'm thinking of doing at college but I can't answer as Carly appears from nowhere and asks me to hold her glass while she gets a plate of food. It's so warm I go to the kitchen and get her some ice. When I come back I see Carly giving him a Christmas kiss but it seems to last a bit too long and John pulls himself away. I laugh and hand her the iced glass. I pull a cracker with John and put on my silly hat. John does the same and I go to say something to him about it when Carly takes my hand and tries to pull me out to dance.

There's a silly dance competition going on but I'm not up for it yet so I watch it all with John beside me. We're laughing at all the shapes being thrown. I stuff handfuls of sausage rolls in my gob. I've got pastry dandruff all down my chin and on my dress. Carly comes over and grabs me by the arm saying, 'Your turn.' I knock a drink over with my other arm on my way. Carly's mum mops it up with some napkins. She don't look too pleased. But I'm in my element now. People are chanting my name and a circle starts to form. I feel myself wobble a bit but I'm ready. I stand there like an Olympic gymnast, arms in the air and all when I spot Carly's brother laugh; he knows I'm going to pull something out the bag. They all know what I'm like after a few drinks. I start to laugh too but get it together before I launch into a full cartwheel across the front room floor. Well, I make the cartwheel but lose my balance standing and have to step back twice, and fall into the Christmas tree. It topples towards Nan sending baubles and stuff all over her. Thank God for the window. It catches the weight and saves the lot from landing on her. So, my dress is up to my crotch and I'm splashed all over the floor, my legs splayed out like a hit and run. The lights on the tree aren't flashing anymore and no one says a thing except Nan going on about me being an utter disgrace or something like that. I look towards her voice and see at least three nans sitting there. My head's all floppy but I aim at the nan in the middle and slur, 'Fuckin' liven up you old stiff,' spraying her with sausage shrapnel to go with all the other shit on top of her. There's a few gasps and some try not to giggle as my head drops down. I can't keep my eyes open and as I drift off all I hear is, 'the bells are ringing out for Christmas day' play out and John, in bits, pissing himself laughing.

Anthony Mellors

Anthony Mellors is Reader in Poetry and Poetics in the School of English at Birmingham City University. His new collection, *The Lewknor Turn*, comes out this year from Shearsman. At present he has no plans to front a new TV series called *Poets Behind Bars*.

Song echt

So if
it was

made plain
to her

song echt
no brain

could you
place it?

Try the
black prairies

that surround
Ely or

the vast
coastal nothingness

at Gedney
Drove End –

This is
flatness to

the point
of obscuring

the coastal
shelf.

Perhaps soon
we'll all

live as
the fenlanders

used to
punting through

sedge between
islands of

quiet habitation.

Sarah-Louise Kearney

Sarah-Louise Kearney is a second-year English and Creative Writing student from Birmingham. She is an aspiring writer who prefers writing prose and is particularly interested in horror and science fiction. She is a keen reader of a variety of genres, and is an orange belt in aikido, a self-defensive martial art. Sarah-Louise also enjoys watching anime.

The House

The supernatural has always been a popular topic in my office. When I first got this job, I thought it'd be a nice change from the retail work I had previously. However, it became just as tiresome. During the four years I've worked here, I've had to endure so many conversations about the supernatural that it's gotten to the point of being ridiculous. I wasn't a big fan, was always sceptical about it, but at first I listened out of kindness. Nowadays I give them a look of interest but really I'm miles away.

Most of this supernatural nonsense stems from an empty house down the road from the office. From what I've heard, it's been abandoned for years. For so long, in fact, that not one living person in the office can remember the previous occupant. Naturally, the house has gone to ruin, with its overgrown garden, broken windows and rotten woodwork. Few people have actually entered inside; too scared to see for themselves what actual 'horrors' lie in store for them. It's no wonder people created stories about the place.

Some are just laughable. More than once, I've had to bite my tongue and suppress my rising laughter. However, I did find it interesting to see people make up these stories just based on the undesirable appearance of the house. The main idea behind them is that the house is inhabited by spirits. There's never a definite number, but there's supposed to be at least one dwelling in the place. And through the years there have been alternative versions of this spirit, each changing his appearance, history and behaviour.

The most popular version states that the spirit wears a hooded raven-black cloak, like the figure of death himself. According to the story, this is so his identity can remain hidden. His only recognisable features are his luminous yellow eyes. Even though people say they have no idea who this spirit is, some believe he was an evil man when alive, with strong ties to the house. Others think he committed a murder there, or was killed for no reason, and now seeks revenge.

Another version suggests the spirit is invisible, just like his identity. Some reckon he was the last occupant of the house and died peacefully in his sleep. They believe the man loved his house too much to leave and so his spirit remained there. He's said to be mischievous, making a great amount of noise according to the night workers. This is because he sees himself as the 'true' owner, so wants the house to be as unattractive as possible to potential buyers.

A more recent version suggests that the spirit has a depressing history. They believe he was a man that was homeless and had a hard life. Orphaned at an early age, and surrounded by bad fortune all his short life, they believe the house was his only source of comfort. This is why he returned there. Some have said they heard all kinds of sobbing.

There have been tales of what has happened to the 'brave and stupid' people that have dared to enter the house. A week ago, one elderly man from my office floor recounted a tale of walking home after a late night at the pub nearby, and noticing a strange hovering figure near the house. Taking a closer look, the man found the figure to be a statue still hovering in the air. This statue seemed to have a striking resemblance to a young man from the office. The week before, he had heard the young man bragging about how he would break into the house and look for valuables. The elderly man suspected the spirit, with his frightening eyes, had the ability to turn men into stone. While everybody reacted to this with gasps of shock, I looked away and rolled my eyes.

Everyone else was repeating it though. One day at lunch a small group of people were retelling the story. I wasn't in the best of moods. My car had broken down, meaning I had to walk in the pouring rain to work. My bag had gotten drenched and all of its contents were sopping wet. The last thing I wanted to hear was this stupid story getting retold again and again.

I walked up to the group and said, 'You honestly don't believe it's true, do you?'

They looked at me, almost astonished that I would dare question it. One member of the group answered, 'Well, what's your opinion of it then?'

'I think it's complete bull. The man obviously had too much to drink. He said himself he was coming back from the pub when he saw this statue.'

'Then explain why the statue looked so much like the guy who broke into the house.'

'They probably bumped into each other, and the man must have been so drunk he thought the guy was a statue. If the guy was breaking into a house, he would have been wearing dark clothing so he wouldn't have been seen properly. Look, this whole spirit business, it's complete crap.'

'Why don't you go into the house then and find out?'

That completely caught me off guard. Everyone thought it was a ridiculous idea to enter the house and would try to dissuade anyone who tried. Even though I didn't believe all the supernatural nonsense, I still wasn't keen on the idea but I didn't want to lose my point in the argument.

'Fine then. I will. I'll go into the house and prove to you all that it's just superstitious nonsense.'

Within a few minutes, the plan was all set. That same night I was to break in, investigate it for the whole night and see if anything would happen. Part of me did think to lie about spending the night there, but my interest in what *was* actually in the house was too overpowering.

The night had come. The azure sky had darkened to ink black with sparkling crystal-like stars. The road was quiet as everyone had left the office, leaving only me standing opposite the house with a torch and cap. It was my last chance to back out. I looked up to the house. Why should I be so worried? It was just a house. I didn't believe in any of the ghost crap and if someone else was able to get in and out of the house, then so should I.

My decision was settled. I would go into the house and I'd have nothing to worry about because there were no spirits inside it. I made my way over to the front garden. The grass had grown long and unruly, while moss had crept over the stone fence. I walked across the weed-strewn path to the front door. It was wooden and perhaps had once been a reddish colour. Now it was a vile dark brown. Before I went in, I put my hair into a ponytail and the cap on my head. The last thing I wanted was bugs in my hair.

The front door creaked open as I pushed it. I was now in the hallway. It was quite dark so I switched my torch on. It had three doors leading to the other rooms and a staircase leading to the next floor. It looked exactly as I had imagined it. The staircase was wooden and rotting. The walls were a depressive grey colour with dark streaks, while the floor was caked with dirt. One of the doors was left ajar so I went into this room first.

It must have been the living area as it contained an old shabby sofa and a fireplace with a thin layer of dust. Upon the fireplace was an ornament. I thought something like an ornament would have been taken or destroyed long ago. It was a black cat figurine, with its body hunched as though ready to pounce. One of its ears was missing which explained why it was never stolen; its value was nothing.

I heard a little knock from somewhere in the house, so I put the ornament back in its place and returned to the hallway. At first I thought the sound had come from the front door. I was wrong. Then there was another knocking. Two little knocks, which came from the very last door. I walked over and pushed it open, even though it resisted. I entered with caution, unsure of what I would find. It appeared to be a kitchen with only broken cabinets. I couldn't find anything that could be making the knocking sounds. I was confused. I knew for definite that I'd heard those noises, but where had they come from? I was so sure it was something in the kitchen.

There it was again. This time I jumped a little as the sound was louder than before. It was followed by three more knocks and I began to notice something move in one of the cabinets. Flashing my torch towards it, I could see a small robin pecking its beak against a wooden panel. I tapped my fingers underneath, and the startled robin flew straight out of the kitchen through a broken window nearby.

There was nothing paranormal about this house. Everything had a rational explanation, people just needed to look for it. Reassured, I looked through the broken window at the back garden. It was similar to the front, just on a larger scale. The grass was overgrown with weeds and nettles. And at the back was a massive oak tree, with its thick branches covering the majority of the garden – making it look darker than it actually was.

I could hear another noise. This time it wasn't anything knocking, it sounded more like muffled footsteps: directly above me. I looked up at the ceiling, wondering what it might be. A small animal perhaps? If a bird had gotten in here, then a cat or fox must have been able to get in as well. Determined to find a rational explanation, I headed towards the staircase.

It didn't look stable and I didn't need to injure myself by making stupid mistakes. As I got to the last step, I heard a floorboard creak. The noise seemed to come from the room in front of me. I walked quietly towards it, expecting to find a small animal inside. But as I got to the door, I heard another sound. A sound I wasn't expecting. Muffled sobbing: it lasted for only a second.

'Hello?' I called out. No response. My curiosity getting the better of me, I entered the room. Nothing. No animal. No person crying. I looked all around and found no one. I couldn't have imagined it, could I? I must have entered the wrong room.

There were two other doors on this floor, with another staircase leading up to the next. I entered the nearest room. There were no windows in here, making it completely dark. I was glad I had my torch with me. With the light, I could see this must have been a bedroom, as it contained a metal bed frame, with a table next to it. A small picture laid flat on the table. Picking it up, I found it was a painting of an old man with peculiar yellow eyes. This explained the glowing eyes of the 'ghost'.

I took a step back, felt a small object underneath my shoe and flashed my torch towards the floor. It was small and triangular, but I couldn't get a good look at it. I bent down to see if I could see it better. The object was either black or grey. Picking it up it felt furry, almost like it belonged to an animal.

'Oh my God!' It was a bloody cat's ear! I dropped it and went straight back downstairs. I didn't want to find the rest of the cat's body.

As I headed for the staircase, I heard a crashing sound.

'Jesus Christ!' This was getting ridiculous now. Someone was setting me up. It was probably someone from that stupid group, trying to get me scared to prove a point. They had probably thrown a brick through one of the windows, and hoped I would run out of the house screaming. Well, I was going to prove my point too, and I was staying put.

I ran down the stairs to find out what had been thrown. I looked in the kitchen and back room finding nothing, but when I returned to the front room I did find something: not what I had expected. The cat ornament had fallen from the fireplace. It was lying in pieces. But how could it have fallen? And then it dawned on me. The ornament was missing an ear.

It was just a big coincidence, that's all it was. But leaving the house was turning out to be a very smart decision. I was still determined to last another few hours at least: I just had to reassure myself there was nothing in the house.

Footsteps sounded above me, on the very top floor; different footsteps, loud and clear and gaining pace. As though someone was running down the stairs. My fear began to grow. I closed the door fast and, using what little strength I had left, attempted to push the sofa in front of the door. It didn't work. I ran to the side of the sofa, hoping I would be hidden somehow. My hands covered my head as each footstep, like a heartbeat, got louder and faster. Then came a loud swinging sound as the door was forced open. I began screaming, expecting a mad man to enter the room and kill me. I was screaming and screaming, but nothing happened.

'Are you ok?'

I opened my eyes. This was not the voice of a mad man. The man before me looked as confused as me. Caught in the moment I began hugging him, so relieved to see he was sane.

'What are you doing in here?' he asked.

I let go of him. 'N-nothing. I could ask the same about you.'

'Well... this'll probably sound stupid, but I got dared to go in here.'

'That's w-weird, I got put into a similar situation,' I said. We couldn't have... had he talked to the same group I had? Did he work at the office too? Just as I was about to put all these questions to him, he started speaking again.

'Are you sure you're ok? You look pale.'

'Yeah I'm fine but – could you walk me back to my house please?' I didn't want to be on my own.

When I got home I hardly slept. I hadn't managed to ask the man any of my questions, I'd been so preoccupied with getting back safely. Throughout the night, I was expecting every kind of noise: a floorboard creak, a crash. Footsteps. They never came.

Once my alarm went off in the morning, I realised I must have dozed off in the early hours, but still felt so tired. I was not looking forward to work.

Throughout the day, I tried to look out for the man from last night, but couldn't find him. It was only at lunchtime that I bumped into one of the group from yesterday.

'How was the ghost hunting last night?'

I twitched a little at the word 'ghost'. I didn't reply, just stared at him.

He dropped his smirk and left me. None of the other members asked me either.

Connor Bloomfield

Connor Bloomfield is a third-year undergraduate whose work is usually rooted in psychogeography and urban landscapes. His literary influences include Sir John Betjeman, Philip Larkin and Pete Doherty, as well as the lyrics of David Bowie, Morrissey and Ian Curtis. He is currently preparing to undertake a Masters degree in English Literature in September.

Twenty Second Century Ghosts

A despondent sigh
Brushes over cold, pulsating air
As Liverpool Street's pavements are
Progressively, malignantly crushed
Under the power of populace.
Now, as we are sealed off, extracted,
Retained under a glass roof,
Where our father asked our third mother:
Could she see it too?

We fester; suffocating insects
And commuters and businessmen
And businesswomen
Gorging on mass produce,
Denying their double existence,
Agreeing to dine on the run.

Revived, we face the platform
Along with our successors.
Stratford, then
Forest Gate, then
Romford, then alight
Onto Essex concrete built on misplaced desires.

Melissa Reynolds-Lawrence

Melissa Reynolds-Lawrence is a self-confessed biblio-phile, freelance copywriter and secret barista. When she isn't buying clothes and books, she's dreaming of it. If she isn't at church or with friends, you'll find her hidden away in a coffee shop, working on her first novel or writing for her blog.

Paris

Sia awoke before her alarm. She sat bolt upright, briefly startled by her unfamiliar surroundings. But she relaxed quickly back into her pillows when she remembered where she was. Paris.

The time on her phone displayed 08:10. She rolled over, contemplating another half an hour or so. She had never been a fan of early starts – with her entire day planned, it seemed a little unnecessary. Breakfast was being served until 09:30. There was no rush.

As Sia weighed up getting out of bed, her phone began to ring. Mason. She quickly cleared her throat, attempting to sound a little livelier.

'Hello?'

'I've called you three times already this morning. What the bloody hell have you been doing?'

Good morning, Mason. I slept beautifully, darling. Thank you.

She rolled her eyes. 'Erm, just getting ready, you know. Drafting articles, going to breakfast in a little while. Nothing unusual.'

'You're still in bed, aren't you?'

Sia threw the covers off, and stalked across the room to the bathroom.

'Don't be ridiculous.' She turned the hot tap on, attempting to open a Clarins Facial Cleanser with her free hand.

She was sure she had heard him tut.

'Whatever. I need your first draft by the end of play. My time.'

'No problem.' Big problem.

'Made much progress on it? I suppose you're hung over. You sound groggy.'

She felt fine. A little giddy but not from two glasses of champagne, surely?

'No, I'm fine. Listen, I've got to go.'

She heard Mason sigh.

'Off sightseeing, are we? Don't get lost. I know what your sense of direction is like.'

'Don't worry about me. I'll probably just find a café or something.' She tried to stave off the excitement that threatened to creep into her voice.

'Don't get carried away. They do some great salads in France, Sia. Right, I'll let you go. End of play, okay?'

'Okay. Love you.'

'Bye.'

She tossed her phone at the bed. It thudded softly as it landed on the black satin duvet cover. Mason was always curt with her on the phone. Sia had brought it up once, and it had been the only time that they had argued. She really had believed that she had been in the right. It couldn't have been so unreasonable to want to hear the words 'I love you', every once in a while, could it? Mason seemed to think this was out of line. For the sake of their relationship, and to keep the peace at work, Sia didn't mention it again. Mason had explained once that yes, he did love her, and if anything changed, he would let her know.

Still in her pyjamas, she sat at the small mahogany desk, ready to get some work done. Taking out her to-do list from the day before, she used the edge of her Filofax to put lines through her completed tasks.

- ~~Write 'first love' article and send to Mason~~
- ~~Impress everyone's socks off at the launch party~~
- ~~Eat pain au chocolat~~
- Visit Eiffel Tower

Only half done. Not the progress she had hoped to make after 24 hours, but progress nonetheless. She had started the article but it was nowhere near being finished. Mason was already getting impatient. Sia was a hard worker, but under Mason, things were tough. She had to work extra hard for his respect at work, so that the rest of the team didn't suspect favouritism – Sia knew better than anyone that that was simply not the case. As soon as Mason became Features Editor, he had changed. He was less affectionate, even outside of work. Sia put it down to stress. It was easier for everyone if she agreed with his ideas, no matter how uncomfortable they made her feel.

Jess and Samantha had agreed to write for the 'First Love' feature. Their stories appealed to *Stiletto* readers. Jess had lost her first love in a car accident, and it had been difficult for her to write about. It was a brave decision to publish it, but the article had received a record-breaking number of responses. Samantha was successfully married to her first love. Now, it was Sia's turn. It didn't seem fair. Her story wasn't remarkable or spectacular. She had thought it was, at the time. Wasn't that the essence of teenage love? Its very fabric was dreams. Mason had been pushing Sia to find a unique tone in her writing. She had never felt she struggled with that until recently. Eventually, she decided that including diary entries was the only *real* way to tell the story. How else could she share the magic of her first encounter with Xavier? Telling the readers how wonderful it was to fall in love at age sixteen was never going to be enough. She was constantly told that she had to 'give more'. Well, there was nothing more to give than her own personal diary entries. She had struggled with the idea for a long time, but it was five years in the past. Mason insisted nobody was going to get hurt. She trusted his judgement. She had to. If she failed, the whole team failed.

With a sigh, she took the leopard print notebook out of her hand luggage. She hadn't dared put it in her actual suitcase. She wasn't even afraid that it would be lost. No – her fear was that it would fall into the wrong hands and someone would read it. She knew it was silly. Even at 22, those anxieties hadn't gone away. Sia flipped it open. The inside cover had butterflies and love hearts doodled all over it in black and pink gel pen. Sia remembered writing 'Property of Sia Matthews' in her best bubble writing, after she bought it in a sale. She ran her fingers down the spiral binding. Maybe she should start writing. But she was hungry, and it was a perfect summer day. In less than a minute, she had managed to talk herself out of working, and decided to head down to breakfast, instead.

Making her way down to the dining room, Sia wondered what her day would be like. She didn't feel nervous, as such. She couldn't put her finger on what the feeling was. It wasn't anxiety. Excitement? Yes, that was it. Sia was excited.

Breakfast was brief. Continental breakfasts in England hadn't ever really appealed to her. The croissants were always a little dry, the orange juice a little too warm. Paris, as expected, had got it just right. Sia was busy reading her emails when a familiar face flashed up on her screen.

'Hello?'

'Sia? Still on for today? I've been looking for you.'

'Oh, I'm at breakfast.'

'So late?' He was still an early bird then.

'Ha. It's only after nine.'

'Think you'll be ready for ten?'

'I thought we said eleven?' He paused on the other end of the phone. She hoped she hadn't put him off.

'It's just... well, I'm excited. You know, to show you a little of Paris.' Sweet relief. He was looking forward to it as much as she was.

'Ha. Okay, ten is fine. See you in a little bit.'

Sia practically ran out of the dining room, to get ready. She looked at the mess of clothes and resisted the urge to tidy up. She'd do it later. What did he have planned for them? She told him she had to leave at five, but it would have to be sooner than that if she was going to finish the article. Damn it, why hadn't she just started it earlier? She had been so distracted. The launch party had taken up all of her thoughts since the moment she landed. As soon as that was over, she had planned to get it out of the way. Find a little café or write out in the courtyard. Things never went to plan when she worked away like this. She thought about cancelling, but she didn't want to seem rude. She hadn't seen Xavier in so long. It seemed ridiculous to pass up the chance to catch up with him. And Mason was right. She would have gotten lost on her own. That was it! She could tell Mason she had headed out to get some writing done and lost her way on the Metro. That would buy her some time.

Standing in the hotel reception, she felt her heart begin to race. Was she really about to do this? *Could* she do this? What if they didn't like each another anymore? She knew it had been a long time, but she still had unanswered questions – questions that she had lived with for over five years now. The same questions that had made her hate him. Or, at least, come close. It had all happened so quickly. She barely had time to get her bearings.

His voice disturbed her thoughts. He was across the way from her, chatting on his phone. How long had he been there? The mauve stripes in the armchair matched his jeans. Had he done that on purpose? She was standing just to the left of him, possibly out of his line of vision. Had he noticed her pass him on her way out of the lift? He looked relaxed and happy, his free arm hanging loosely down the side of the chair. His brown hair was shorter than usual. The back rested just on the collar of his grey shirt. Sia was a little lost in watching him, when suddenly, he put his phone down and turned around. He was looking right at her.

'You're here.'

He took her hand and leaned down to kiss her cheek. She suddenly felt young again. Very young. Smaller, even. Vulnerable. The pep talk she had given herself in her suite echoed in her ears.

Frozen to the spot, she couldn't think of a single word to say. Don't lose your cool, Sia. Hold it together.

'So, what do you want to do? I had a couple of things in mind.' Still nothing. Why couldn't she speak?

'Tower?' Her voice was high-pitched, nowhere near as calm as she wanted.

'Great. Mind if we walk? We're so close and the weather is gorgeous.' He picked up the pace a little, and headed for the automatic doors.

It was busier than she had expected for so early in the day. She had imagined that tourists wouldn't be heading out until around lunchtime. Or maybe that was just *her*. They strolled side by side, weaving their way through couples, and stepping aside for children who had run up the street, ahead of their parents. Xavier had never really been a fan of idle chitchat. Their conversation consisted mostly of work, but it was easy.

'So, you were freelance before *Stiletto*?'

'Yeah. It was mostly blogging but I did get an article featured in *Company*. Obviously a huge deal.'

'I know.'

'You read *Company*?'

He laughed but then paused. 'No. Of course not. I was so impressed when I saw it. My friend told me about it.'

'Oh, it was nothing special.'

Sia still had several copies of the issue that she featured in. They were locked away in her memory box. It had only been a career article but she had felt proud.

'I was a little bit proud, you know. Sort of cheering you on from a distance.'

As they turned the corner, the buzz of tourists chatting had gotten louder. Sia had never been able to imagine how gorgeous The Eiffel Tower would be in real life. She had got so used to seeing it on photos and postcards. She couldn't believe it was right in front of her.

'Do you want to go up?' Xavier was standing with his hand on the curve of Sia's spine. She felt a tingle. She had to look up to answer him. He seemed taller today. Maybe because she was wearing flat shoes.

'You know, I've only ever wanted to see it up close. But we can go up, if you like. I don't mind.'

Xavier paused and looked over at the queue of tourists. Most in shorts or dresses, with their cameras hanging around their necks. Ice cream in one hand, phrase book in another. Some were holding gift bags, where they had bought key rings and postcards of the Eiffel Tower.

'No. I've been up before. It's pretty special at night though.' Sia looked up at it again, standing on tiptoes to see the top.

'I can imagine.'

They were strolling again. Arm in arm, this time. Xavier insisted she stayed close in case of pickpockets.

'Well, you can cross the Eiffel Tower off your to-do list now.' Sia turned her head to look at him. She raised an eyebrow as she looked into his eyes. Blue and playful.

'How did you know that was on the list?'

He laughed. 'Sia, the whole time I've known you, you've made lists of everything. There's no way you would have come to Paris without making one.'

He was right. All this time... she had thought he would have forgotten all about her. But he was still the same. Thoughtful. And so was she. Well, her habits at least.

'Can't believe you would remember something so odd.'

'It's not odd. It's inspiring. I started to do the same. Look.' He took his phone out of his pocket. 'There are apps for it. It's amazing.'

Sia laughed. He was still the same when he was excited about something. His smile reached a little further and his face lit up brighter than usual. Then his brow furrowed.

'What's wrong?' Was it his girlfriend? Did he even have one?

'Bugger. Work. I'm so sorry, Sia. An exec that I was meant to be interviewing for the issue is flying out of Paris today.'

She knew all this fun was too good to be true. 'Oh. That's not a problem, is it? Don't you have staff out here?'

'I do, but it was meant to be me. I'm so sorry.'

'Don't worry about it. You're important. These things happen.' She hoped she had hidden the disappointment in her voice.

Back in her suite, Sia had barely let the lock click on the door before she called Frankie. If there was anyone who would be excited for her, it would be her best friend.

'How's it going? Haven't bumped into the ex again, have we?'

'Not exactly bumped into, no.'

'Sia? What are you not telling me?'

'Nothing.'

'Spit it out.'

'Okay, everything. And it's been killing me.'

'Oh gosh. So, you spoke to him at the party, and then what?'

'Well, I went to bed after the launch and he text me.'

'Saying what? That it was great to see you? He liked your arse in your dress?'

'No. He just, you know, offered to show me around Paris.'

'Just Paris?' Francesca barely stifled a snigger.

'Shut up. It was a great idea. Who better to show me around France than a real life French man?'

'Sisi, he's only half French. And secondly, France is full of handsome French m –'

'– Hear me out.'

'– And thirdly, are we forgetting that he broke your heart?'

'We were just kids. He explained all of that and –'

'– And my fourthly, I don't even know if that's a word but my point is that you have a boyfriend. A shit one but he *is* your boyfriend.'

Sia realised that she had almost entirely forgotten about

Mason. She checked her work-phone but nothing. Not even a missed call.

'Sia? Are you there? What's wrong?'

Francesca's voice shattered her thoughts.

'Nothing. I'm, I'm fine. Just tired. Paris is a busy city, you know.'

'Have you heard from Mason at all? Did he know that Xavier was going to become editor?'

Of course he didn't know. Or did he? Would he have told her, if he did know? It must have slipped his mind.

'Oh, probably. But you know what he's like. Doesn't tell me anything unless it's important.'

'Yeah. I hadn't meant to sound harsh. I'll let you get off. Skype later?'

'Yeah. Course. It's fine. No worries. Bye, Frankie.'

Sia flopped back onto the bed and let her head sink into the pillows. Looking up at the delicately painted ceiling, she felt a single tear fall down her cheek into her hair. Sitting up, she reached over for a tissue. Her phone vibrated.

Sorry I had to dash. Dinner tonight? Xavi… xx

She knew she should say no.

Yes please… x

Michèle Barzey

Michèle Barzey is a writer and theologian who explores how the creative, theological and political spheres interact and inform each other. Her writing, examples of which can be found at http://afrobehnpoet.wordpress.com/, blurs the boundaries between poetry, prose and drama. She is currently working on *Dancing the Dark Tango,* a poetic memoir of depression.

Dancing the Dark Tango
A Memoir

The walking dead aren't the shambling, shuffling zombies of your childhood nightmares. Nor are they the sexy, seducing vampires of your night-time fantasies. We are the ones who continue to walk among you even when the flame of hope has died. None of you know which of your actions snuffed out the last spark. Was it dammed by faint praise or knocked out with a fist? Or was it the draught of the front door as you walked out on your child?

* * *

When it comes to giving medals for achievement, getting out of bed isn't at the top of the list. Some days I haven't managed it at all and on others it's taken me hours. On the 'easier' days I don't feel anything, except a despair so profound that getting out of bed is the least of my worries. On a bad day I will argue with myself for hours trying to force myself to move. If after two or three hours I manage it, there will be no respite. I will harangue myself for wasting so much time, then I'll switch on the radio and I can stop goading and yelling at myself because David Cameron, Atos and their ilk are quite happy to do it for me.

* * *

Duck Moments

Don't judge me.
I may look lazy
on the outside
but inside
I'm paddling like crazy.

* * *

Darkness isn't the enemy. Darkness is what numbs you so the pain doesn't kill you. Darkness takes away the light that exposes you and hides the look of disgust on others' faces when they see what you are really like. Darkness frees you to talk to your therapist.

* * *

Dark nights and empty dreams
Lost hopes and broken promises
Hollow hearts and twisted lives

* * *

Judas Christ

The peace you promised never came
You give a glimpse then slam the door

* * *

The puppeteer decrees it and it is so. With careless abandon he throws his creations into the air, not caring where or how they land. As their blood flows, he cuts the strings and leaves them sprawled and broken, abandoned dolls pitched out of a cosmic pram during a swiftly passing tantrum.

* * *

One of the side-effects of spending time in a psychiatric hospital is the way that your perceptions of normality change without you realising it. Months, or even years later, I'll be talking to someone and they'll give me a look and I'll know that they've put me in the OMG section of their mind.

* * *

I Remember

Whenever I eat carrot cake I remember summertime
picnics in Pype Hayes park, mad friends drinking cider
pushing back the dark times with talk and laughter.

and then,

I remember the thick fog of the smoking room,
the stodgy food and the late night TV,
the long nights and the card playing days.

and then,

I remember the walks around the grounds,
lying on the grass, my life on hold as time
circled by and the abnormal became the norm.

and then,

I remember two months passing after the suicide.
Two months before I realised my first thought should
not have been, 'Lucky sod, how'd he manage that?'

and then,

I remember the walks around the grounds
not seeing the trees, or the squirrels playing tag
seeing only sharp edges and the potential for ending.

* * *

50 Shades

I didn't like the book but I could see why so many people found the thought of being submissive attractive. It's what hospital does to you. I don't know whether it's intentional or a natural side-effect of living in an institution. You're told what you can and can't do. A routine is set up for you. Someone else decides when you get up, eat, take your tablets and go to ward round. Nothing is required of you. You have no decisions to make. Your clothes are few and you wash them when they're dirty. The rest of the time you sit in front of the TV and zone out.

When your life has become an elaborate chess game and you can no longer keep all the moves in your head. When it can take an hour to decide what to eat, and another to decide what to wear or whether to shower. When every decision needs to be thought through in case you make the wrong one. When the consequence of making the wrong choice is never articulated but you live in constant dread of it happening, it's a relief to have someone else make the decisions.

* * *

Admittance

The second time I saw my psychiatrist she locked me up. I don't think I gave much of a protest. There was no point. I didn't really care what happened to me and I was sure that when she said, 'I'd like you to stay a while,' it was more than a suggestion. I said I needed to go and get some clothes. She looked at me and I knew she knew I wasn't intending to come back. She suggested that I call someone to fetch things for me. I don't know who called or what was said but my boss and his wife came and got my keys and left me there. I don't remember much else about that first day except sitting in a chair staring blankly at a TV screen.

That first night on the ward I drew the curtains around my

bed. I lay staring at the ceiling but I didn't sleep. They kept looking through the curtains and asking me if I was alright. Bloody stupid question. I lay there staring into the dark so tired and so out of it. They gave me sleeping tablets the next night but that simply exchanged one darkness for the other.

The darkness is hard to describe. Sometimes it's your friend. In the dark you are not exposed, your hurts and agonies are not raw and open to any passing gaze. Sometimes you would give your life to sink into that darkness and carry on sinking for all eternity.

Sometimes the darkness is feral. It sets your hair on edge and you can feel it prowling around the edges of your mind. Whispering, always whispering. Sometimes barely audible, but always unsettling and undermining. You try to ignore its voice but you can't because the beast is you and the beast knows how to hurt. No matter how bruising your mum's words were, they are nothing to this. This constant ripping apart of self. And the pain. The pain is unbearable and their tablets don't even touch it. How can they? You are being ripped apart from the inside out and there's no painkiller for that.

And it doesn't show on the outside. You are screaming so loud, but when they check on you all they can see is someone lying in bed staring at the ceiling.

I was torn between the darkness that comforted and the Darkness that tormented, and so for a time I became nothing. I did what I was told, I took tablets and answered questions and tried not to be.

* * *

I've Stopped to Listen

I've stopped.
To listen to the voices is more than I can bear.
They mutter constantly, quietly, subtly.

They suck me dry and drown out
the voices of those who try to reach me.

I've stopped.
In this ward, I will no longer be.
I will wake and I will walk
but I will not be me.

* * *

In winter, when I walked through the grounds, I saw death in the bare trees and envied the leaves.

* * *

Touching the past
Stroking the gravestone

* * *

Death

Death is my oldest friend. I've known him since I was about nine. One of my earliest memories is of walking with him on my way to school. I'd just passed the baker's when he caught up with me. I didn't plan how to leave with him, that came later, but there was a certainty that the only way to stop the pain would be to follow him. I remember the rain, and the way it cried for me so that I didn't have to. I think that's why I've always loved the rain. There's nothing more comforting than lying indoors listening to the rain drumming on the windows or more reassuring than a thunderstorm overhead.

* * *

Why do you say that suicide is the coward's way out?   When the ancient mariners saw 'here be dragons' and still sailed off into the sunset, were they cowards? How much more brave is it to dive into the last unknown?

* * *

Suicide

The first week I was in Highcroft a man committed suicide. He was a new admission and had sat next to me in the TV room all that afternoon. I hadn't spoken to him; in fact I hadn't spoken to anyone since my admission. I don't remember anything about him except that he was white and had brown hair. When the alarm went off I thought there was a fire. It wasn't until later that I heard some of the other patients talking and realised he'd hung himself in the bathroom. There was no shock or horror, just a touch of envy and a mild curiosity as to how he'd managed to get away with it.

* * *

Don't Go Gently

Why the hell not?
The tide of days
pounds at my being
Eroding all sense of who I am.

You lied about the Light.
You said He'd bring me peace.

You never spoke about the night.
The black warmth.
The warm silence.
The silent end.
An end to fear and doubt
and shame and guilt.

How dare you forbid me the night.

The night calls to me.
'Celebrate the bringing of my darkness
Surrender to the healing in my dark.
Slip into the peace of my darkness.'

Oh I welcome,
will always welcome the dying of the light.
And I will go gentle
Oh so gentle into that good night.

* * *

Between wanting to die and planning my death there was an intermediary period when I played games like 'Tablet Russian Roulette'. Whenever I had a headache I'd take too many tablets and see what happened. Or I'd take a few too many anti-depressants and sleeping tablets. The problem with trying to make your suicide look accidental is that it becomes complicated and the chances of things going wrong increases dramatically. If the Paracetamol overdose doesn't kill you straight away, you can die painfully days later due to liver failure. I didn't want to die in pain nor did I want to end up incapacitated and unable to kill myself.

People say suicide is selfish. I was quite considerate. I tried to think of ways that wouldn't involve other people. I ruled out stepping in front of a train or a car because it wasn't fair on the driver or any witnesses. I worried about who would find the body and whether they would be traumatised for life.

When I was a child I saw a woman catch fire. It was during the 'Winter of Discontent' when it seemed as if everyone was on strike. In the alley that sliced halfway through my road a mound of rubbish had been piling up for weeks. We were coming home from school one night, when the woman who lived in the house next to the alley burst out of her door and began yelling about how she couldn't stand the smell and the rats anymore.

All I can remember is a small piece of blackened paper with red sparks, still glowing, floating across the road and landing in front of me. Nothing else.

I blanked out her pouring petrol on the pile and setting it on fire, the sounds she must have made when she realised that she had spilt some petrol on her clothes, the sounds of the sirens and the commotion that goes with any emergency. The only things I couldn't blank out were that piece of paper, waking up screaming from a recurring nightmare where I'd be in an underground maze running from a giant fireball, and a fear of fire that lasted for years. I couldn't bear to be the cause of someone else's nightmare.

Suicide is only selfish in the sense that finally you can do something for yourself. If the only reason you're alive is because you're worrying how your death will affect other people there comes a point when that's not enough of a deterrent and you decide, 'I want this.' When that happens, the voices stop whispering so you're calm enough to plan. Your indecision goes away and you're left with a bleak certainty that you're doing the right thing.

* * *

I emptied out the containers and blister packs of Venlafaxine, Ibuprofen, Paracetamol, Seroxat and Asprin. I don't know why it was important, but I lined up the empty containers and sorted the pills into size and colour. First the rows of white round tablets, then the green and cream capsules and finally the large orange Smartie look-a-likes. I poured a glass from the bottle of Bushmills and stared at the rows. When the doorbell rang later that night, the whisky had gone but the tablets were still there.

* * *

Dear Life

By the time you read this
I'll have danced the Dark Tango

I'll have stood in the spotlight
and looked to the dark

the floor will have emptied
and a silence descended

my feet will have beat out
the rhythm of death.

By the time you read this
I'll have danced the Dark Tango

I'll have signalled the band
that it's time to begin

I'll have crossed the dance floor
to meet my last partner

I'll have taken His hand
and moved into His arms.

By the time you read this
I'll have danced the Dark Tango

my dress will be scarlet
and my heart will have slowed

He'll have drained my life blood
as we circled the floor.

By the time you read this
I'll have danced the Dark Tango

I'll have danced the Dark Tango
and left with my Night.

* * *

Self-harm is like domestic violence. It sounds more innocent
than it is.

* * *

the first time

she says to me what happened to your arm i say have you ever
tried to stop a cat fight she laughs we talk she leaves i trace the
scars on my arm and remember and remember

a hospital bed in a green curtained womb the soon to be familiar
blade the propitiously red robe which deepened when my blood
flowed free theyre right you know the first cut is the deepest
you dont know how itll hurt like hell for a time theres nothing
but the pain and the burning and the blood so the next time you
steel yourself for the burning and the pain the next time you
look forward to the relief and the release and the surprise the
surprise when your arm opens up and you find that your blood
is beautiful and rich and red and not the oozing green pus youd
thought was seeping from your soul
   and now in the time when i dont i miss the cutting not the
pain but the blood when your arm opens up and the drops start
to flow and the drops start to flow slowly and the drops start
to flow slowly together and the drops are beautiful the drops

are rich and the drops are red it was never about the pain god knows im not a masochist the pain was the obstacle the pain was the race the blood was the prize when i had the courage to cut deep the blood poured out and proved i was human the blood poured out and purged my demons and purged my demons for a while the blood poured out and purged my demons purged my demons for a while

Blades

It took a while to find the right blade for cutting. My first was one which I took out of a ladies razor. I remember sitting on the grass outside the ward trying to break open the plastic covering to get at it. The blade was too narrow to get a proper grip so after that first time I looked for another. However, it served its purpose and left me with my most visible scar.

My second was a razor blade but I didn't like the feel of it. It was too thin and when you cut, it stung. Also you ended up with small cuts on your thumb and forefinger which could be painful if you were eating salty chips.

My third and final was a Stanley knife blade (other utility blades are available!). It was the right thickness and size to hold and was not as painful as the others. I kept it in a matchbox by the side of my bed and have never got round to throwing it away.

* * *

blade

she clung to me
and held on
as if by letting go
her life
would drift away

she gazed at me and

in her eyes i saw myself
sharp
and silver
and streaked with red

she caressed me gently and as gently
as you'd wipe away a tear
she wiped away
her blood

she set me down on the side
lit the candles poured the wine
rich
and red
and reminiscent

she uncovered herself
and as she stepped into the bath
in the shimmering light
i glimpsed the traces of my love

she held me
and as her tears bled into the water
i drank her sorrow
long
and slow
and deep

she held me
and as her blood flowed into the foam
she drank her merlot
long
and slow
and deep

Matthew R. Ford

Matthew R. Ford has written and directed *Losing Innocence*; a feature film, and a short film, *Hurt*, that was nominated for 'Best Festival Short' at the 2012 MVSA Awards. He is currently working on various stage productions, a TV pilot, and developing a new feature-length screenplay.

Redundant

Scene 7

Bedroom. Morning. The alarm clock sounds.

Jennifer awakens. She looks tired, hasn't slept well. She looks beside her, Elliot is not in the bed.

The alarm clock persists. It grows in volume. Louder. Louder.

Jennifer throws the clock across the room, breaking it against the wall.

Elliot walks in, dressed for work.

Jennifer lies back down, her face partially buried in the pillow.

> JENNIFER
> An early start today?

Elliot doesn't respond. He notices the shattered pieces of the alarm clock on the floor.

> ELLIOT
> What did you do that for?

> JENNIFER
> It was annoying me.

> ELLIOT
> You couldn't hit snooze?

> JENNIFER
> Perhaps I didn't want to snooze.

> ELLIOT
> It's broken.

                    JENNIFER
                    (Raised)
          Perhaps I didn't want to snooze Elliot…
          perhaps I didn't want to wake up (beat)
          at least not as…

She checks herself.

                    ELLIOT
          Aren't you going into work?

                    JENNIFER
          You're oblivious aren't you? (beat)
          Either that, or you really don't care.

Elliot studies the clock in his hands, playing
with it in vain, trying to fix it.

                    ELLIOT
          What are you talking about Jenny?

                    JENNIFER
          Would you cheat on me?

Her question catches him off guard.

                    ELLIOT
          What?

                    JENNIFER
          It's a simple enough question. (beat)
          Would — you — cheat — on — me?

                    ELLIOT
          Don't be stupid… of course not. No.

                    JENNIFER
          But then… you're bound to say that…
          aren't you?

Silence.

                    JENNIFER
                    (Softly)
          I've cheated on you.

Silence.

Elliot puts the clock down on the table next to
his pillow.

Jenny's voice is soft. She keeps herself turned
away from Elliot. As she speaks, her eyes glaze
and her voice falters.

> ELLIOT
>
> Jenny?

> JENNIFER
>
> It's true. It was just after you lost
> your job.

Elliot doesn't know how to react. He just sits and
listens, facing the wall.

Jennifer recounts the story like a reminiscence.

> JENNIFER
>
> He was… (beat) well, he wasn't you…
> that's all that matters isn't it? I was
> shopping, buying dinner when I called
> you to see if you fancied steak, I
> think, or lamb. You answered and said
> you were going out, to the pub. It
> sounded like you were already there. I'd
> only left the house ten minutes before I
> called, which means you must have left
> as soon as I was out of the way. I just…
> wandered around the aisles, putting back
> everything I had picked up like some
> (laughs) insane woman. (Pause) Then I saw
> him… well… he saw me, I guess. We were
> in the vegetable aisle, I was putting
> back a bag of rocket salad… the last one
> and he wanted to buy it.

She pauses for a while. Elliot doesn't move.

> JENNIFER
>
> He made me… nervous… he looked at me like
> you used to look at me, and I remembered
> how I felt… how that felt… I felt… (beat)

> weak. When he asked me my name, I lied.
> I don't know why, I just made one up.
> It felt better if I wasn't me, if I was
> somebody else… if he thought I wasn't
> who I am.

Elliot turns to look at his wife. He is silent.
Jennifer is still facing away from him.

> JENNIFER
> When I got home that night… you were
> still out. (Pause) I don't know what
> time you got back.

Elliot tries to remember the night his wife is
talking about.

> ELLIOT
> Where did you…?

> JENNIFER
> (Interrupting)
> Does it matter? Would it change anything
> if I fucked him in our bed, in this bed?
> Or on the stairs, in the kitchen, the
> car, at his place?

Elliot swallows hard, the thought of his wife with
another man.

Silence.

The blurred image and soft panting sounds reappear
in the window space.

> JENNIFER
> It was here… right here, where I'm lying
> now. I lay here, while you were out and I
> let him creep on top of me and I guided
> his hands over every inch of my body.
> I felt him… inside me, his breath, his
> weight, his smell… all of him. (Beat)
> and when I opened my eyes… he was gone.

Elliot can't speak. He can't move.

The window space is empty.

>   JENNIFER
> When I woke up… you were snoring next to
> me. Oblivious. I made you some breakfast
> and had a shower and went to work, and
> everywhere I went, every time I closed my
> eyes… he was there. (Beat) I can close
> them now and still taste his kiss.

Jennifer closes her eyes: her fingers tenderly
stroke her lips. A tear rolls down her face.

Elliot pulls her over to face him.

>   ELLIOT
> Have you seen him since? Have you seen
> him again?

Jennifer opens her eyes and stares straight into
Elliot's.

>   JENNIFER
> Every time I close my eyes…

>   ELLIOT
> I don't… I don't… why, Jenny? How can
> you…

>   JENNIFER
> It's what I wanted.

>   ELLIOT
> You wanted to cheat on me?

>   JENNIFER
> Yes. I wanted to, I wanted to feel
> wanted, desired… touched, loved…

Silence

>   JENNIFER
> But I couldn't.

>   ELLIOT
> You… couldn't? But you just said…

                    JENNIFER
                   (Shouting)
     I just said I wanted to… Elliot. I
     closed my eyes and I had him, I opened
     my eyes and he was gone and that fantasy
     was what I had… is what I have (pause)
     instead of you.

                    ELLIOT
     What are you saying? You imagined this?
     It was a dream? What the fuck are you
     doing to me Jenny? What are you trying
     to do to me?

                    JENNIFER
     Does it matter if it was a dream? Does
     it matter if he wasn't here, lying where
     you do every night? I still felt what I
     felt… it was still him making me feel
     it. Not you. Not us. It was him… and
     me… it was ours and it had nothing to do
     with you… nothing to do with my husband.

                    ELLIOT
     Jenny, it was a fucking fantasy! Are
     you insane? You lead me to believe that
     you've been cheating on me… you tear my
     fucking heart out and then tell me that
     it was all a fucking… that you imagined
     it all? That it wasn't real!

                    JENNIFER
     I'm telling you what I felt… up here,
     inside me… and it wasn't you.

Silence

                    JENNIFER
     It's never you.

                    ELLIOT
     What do you mean, it's never me?

> JENNIFER

When you close your eyes… who am I?

> ELLIOT

What?

> JENNIFER

Just answer the fucking question Elliot…
stop stalling, stop playing dumb.

> ELLIOT

You're you… you're… Jenny, you're making
no sense. You wake up, smash the clock
to pieces and then start telling me you
cheated on me in a dream…

> JENNIFER
>   (Interrupting)

In a fantasy…

> ELLIOT

Whatever, it's the same fucking thing.

> JENNIFER

Are you working late tonight?

The question stops Elliot dead.

> JENNIFER

It's a simple question Elliot, they're
all simple questions. You just complicate
them with your lack of answers.

Silence.

> JENNIFER

Are you?

Silence.

> ELLIOT

Do you want me to?

Jennifer gets out of bed.

> JENNIFER

I can't do this anymore.

She turns her back on Elliot and leaves the room.
Elliot turns to the window. A magpie lands in the
tree.

Scene 8

Bedroom. Dark. The Red Lamp flickers on. Elliot
stands next to it, watching it, drawn to it like a
moth to a flame.

The Red Purse sits on the bedside table; he picks
it up and opens it. He takes out a small passport-
sized photograph.

> RED HEADED WOMAN
(Off)

    We're past the point of no return.

Elliot turns around, startled.

The Red Headed Woman walks in, around to the
opposite side of the Bed, Elliot's side. She faces
him. A drink in her hand, a glass of bourbon.

Elliot places the picture back in her purse. She
takes it off him and puts it back on the table.

> ELLIOT
> I only have the one picture y' know.

The Red Headed Woman looks uninterested. She
lights up a cigarette.

> ELLIOT
> After the baby… (pause)… I threw
> everything out. I thought it would help,
> I thought it would make a clean slate,
> a fresh start. They're just memories…
> the pictures, they were just reminders
> of that life. (Beat) I even trashed the
> Video Camera.

Silence. Elliot looks over to The Red Headed
Woman, she appears bored.

> ELLIOT
> Now I just remember things how I want to remember them… not necessarily how they happened.

Silence.

The Red Headed Woman stubs out her cigarette and gazes into nothing. Her face changes. For the first time, she looks nostalgic, lost in a memory. Emotion trails her face.

Silence.

> RED HEADED WOMAN
> I used to have photographs.

She winces in pain and brings her hand up to her head.

> ELLIOT
> Are you ok?

She motions him to stay away and composes herself.

> RED HEADED WOMAN
> I had pictures (beat) of my daughter.

Elliot stays silent, allowing her to open up in the space.

> RED HEADED WOMAN
> I used to keep them in a heart-shaped box, it was always next to the bed.

She strokes the empty space on the bedside table.

> RED HEADED WOMAN
> I never framed them, or hung them up on the walls, or put them into an album… they were mine, (beat) not to share.

Elliot remains silent. Unsure.

> RED HEADED WOMAN
> She's still alive… if that's what you were wondering?

                         ELLIOT
           I… I just…

                    RED HEADED WOMAN
                         (Interrupting)
           She doesn't speak to me anymore. Hasn't
           for… years.

The Red Headed Woman laughs and lights another
cigarette. She watches the smoke circle in front
of her, gently waving her hand through it.

                    RED HEADED WOMAN
           I think… (pause)… I think maybe, it was
           my fault. I think perhaps… I wanted it
           to be (beat) I hoped it was…

Elliot looks uncomfortable. He adjusts his
collar, feeling hot. The Red Headed Woman remains
transfixed on the smoke spiralling in front of her.

                         ELLIOT
           Should I go?

The Red Headed Woman spins around to face him.

                    RED HEADED WOMAN
           Go? You want to go? Now?

                         ELLIOT
           I just thought…

                    RED HEADED WOMAN
           What? That it would be easier for you to
           leave and turn your back on this?

                         ELLIOT
           No.

                    RED HEADED WOMAN
           You wanted this… remember? It was you who
           came to me. You could have stayed with
           your wife but you didn't, you wanted me,
           and now the moment it gets… real… you
           want to go?

                    ELLIOT
          Real? I just thought that… what can I
          do?

                    RED HEADED WOMAN
          What choice have you got?

                    ELLIOT
          Choice?

                    RED HEADED WOMAN
          Could you choose?

                    ELLIOT
          You're making no sense? Choose? Choose
          what?

                    RED HEADED WOMAN
          You can't have us both. Did you think
          it would just go on like this forever?
          You wake up with her and fuck me before
          bedtime?

                    ELLIOT
          Jenny?

                    RED HEADED WOMAN
          Yes — Jenny. Remember her?

                    ELLIOT
          You're…

                    RED HEADED WOMAN
                    (Interrupting)
          Making no sense?

Silence. Elliot looks taken aback.

The Red Headed Woman turns away from Elliot. She
speaks slowly, deliberately.

                    RED HEADED WOMAN
             Do you know what rejection is?

Silence.

Elliot sits slumped on the bed, his back to her.

> RED HEADED WOMAN
> Do you know what it is to reject somebody
> and what it does to them? To leave
> them… alone… in this place, to fend for
> themselves and deal with everything on
> their own. No support, nobody to turn
> to, knowing that who they are isn't good
> enough?

She turns to Elliot who senses it. He turns to
face her.

> RED HEADED WOMAN
> It can destroy a person.

They hold each other's gaze for a moment, then the
Red Headed Woman gets up and slowly leaves the
bedroom.

Darkness.

Scene 9

Elliot and Jennifer's bedroom. Morning.

Jennifer is stood gazing out of the window, still
in her bedclothes. Lost.

She watches a Magpie flutter to a landing in the
trees.

The Red Purse lies discarded in the centre of the
bed, an anomaly in the otherwise neat room. Elliot
enters, looking tired, carrying two cups of tea.
He spots the purse.

> ELLIOT
> Are you ok? You've been standing there
> all morning.

Silence.

Elliot puts the two cups down next to the bed on
Jennifer's side.

He pauses to look at the purse.

Jennifer remains fixated on the window.

> JENNIFER
> I can see right through myself.

> ELLIOT
> Jen?

> JENNIFER
> I can see my reflection (beat) in the
> window (beat) but it's… transparent. I
> can see the world beyond it, the grass,
> the trees, the sky. It's all (beat)
> there. I'm just a blurred mirage layered
> against it.

Elliot sits down on the bed, watching his wife.

> ELLIOT
> I made you a cup of tea.

> JENNIFER
> I don't know if that means there's more
> to me (pause) or if I'm disappearing.

> ELLIOT
> It will get cold.

Silence. There is an unnerving pause.

> JENNIFER
> What does she give you that I don't?

Elliot looks at the purse.

There is a calmness, an acceptance in Jennifer's
voice, as if her emotion has reached a plateau.

> ELLIOT
> Who?

> JENNIFER
> You know who Elliot…

She turns to look at her husband.

> JENNIFER
> We're past the point of no return.

She turns back to the window.

> JENNIFER
> One of the most important things in my
> job is listening. I hear (beat) all sorts
> of things but it's only sometimes that
> I actually… listen. My time, that space
> where people tell me their insides…
> nothing ever leaves there, nothing.
> (Beat) It never comes out of there
> with me, not really. I leave it there,
> locked up, out of sight, filed away… only
> revisiting it again when they come back
> with their issues, when their problems
> come back into my life arrogantly
> assuming they're welcome (beat) but I
> don't really listen to them, I hear them.

> ELLIOT
> Jen, come on, we'll go downstairs and
> make some breakfast, and just spend the
> day in front of the TV. We're both…

> JENNIFER
> (Interrupting sharply)
> Both?

Her interruption provokes silence again. It sits
there between them, as she remains lost in the
window.

The purse screams in the middle of the room.

> JENNIFER
> Every day since you've met me you've
> been falling out of love with me.

> ELLIOT
> That's not true.

> JENNIFER
> Change is inevitable, everything
> is always changing… all the time.

>   Constantly. Why should your feelings be
>   any different?

>   ELLIOT
>   They're not.

>   JENNIFER
>   So, you're finally being honest?

>   ELLIOT
>   I just… I wish it was like it was before.

>   JENNIFER
> You lost your job Elliot, it's hardly a reason to
> leave me.

>   ELLIOT
>   Now who's not being honest?

>   JENNIFER
>   So it is? You are?

>   ELLIOT
>   I never said that.

>   JENNIFER
>   You never say anything Elliot…

>   ELLIOT
>   (Interrupting)
>   It's what I mean that interests you.

> Silence.

>   JENNIFER
>   In all of this, why am I the only person
>   who feels redundant? (Long pause) I feel
>   like a stranger in my own life.

> She turns away from the window for the first time.

> Elliot faces her.

> She looks at the purse.

>   JENNIFER
>   Tell me what it is.

                    ELLIOT
        You're not the only one who feels
        redundant Jenny.

                    JENNIFER
        I need you… you don't need me. I'd say
        I'm pretty fuckin' redundant.

Elliot turns away.

                    ELLIOT
        Do you think we'd be better off… humans I
        mean… without emotion?

                    JENNIFER
        We'd be robots.

                    ELLIOT
        Would we? Do you know that lions, lions
        will mate with whichever female is in
        heat, not sticking to any one mate… if
        more than one is in heat, then he'll
        mate with however many he can.

                    JENNIFER
        Elliot, just tell me… if you're out of
        love with me, if you're… (faltering)
        if you don't look at me and find me
        attractive, just…

                    ELLIOT
                (Interrupting)
        Jenny… listen to what I'm saying…
        listen to what I mean. (Beat) Listen
        to me. (Pause) They mate with however
        many they can, to reproduce. The whole
        purpose is to carry on the population
        of that pride… those Lions, they do it
        to leave a legacy. (Beat) They serve a
        purpose. It has nothing to do with love,
        attachment… emotion. The lionesses, they…
        they respond to his dominance, there's
        usually only one mating male per pride;
        because they know… they know what it is

for. They are all part of this circle —
of life. They all serve a purpose.

                    JENNIFER
            (Quietly, through tears)
        Just say what you want to say Elliot.

                    ELLIOT
        When I lost my job, I lost the last
        remaining part of me that served any
        real purpose. (Beat) I couldn't provide
        for you… I couldn't be somebody that you
        looked up to, that you could depend on.
        (Pause) I couldn't even give you what
        you wanted the most.

Silence.

                    JENNIFER
        A child? (Beat) Is that what this is
        about?

Elliot hangs his head.

                    ELLIOT
        Every time I look at you, I see my own
        life accelerating past me. It's moving
        so quickly, I think it might leave me
        behind. I'm still… I'm still that boy
        you met eight years ago, I'm not the man
        I should be. (Beat) I'm not the man that
        you should have.

Jennifer moves closer to him but he edges away
slightly, enough to make her freeze her steps.

                    ELLIOT
        It's easier… to hide behind the things
        that don't matter. They don't move or
        change because they are obsolete, (beat)
        you can stay hidden behind them forever
        if you want. It's the things that do
        matter that change, that move forward.
        You can't hide behind those things,

>   you can't ignore them because if you
>   do, they're gone and you're left… left
>   behind with all the things that are…
>   irrelevant. All the things that are…

>   JENNIFER
>   (Interrupting)
>   Redundant.

Elliot holds his hand out slightly behind him, his
head still bowed.

Jennifer reaches out and rests the tips of her
fingers against his.

>   JENNIFER
>   I can't let you see her anymore.

Slowly, she leaves the room.

After a moment, Elliot turns around and looks at
the Red Purse lying on the bed. He picks it up and
thinks for a moment and then leaves the room.

Danielle Cotton

Danielle Cotton was born in Birmingham in early 1991. She started school in 1995, where a pen was put in her hand, and she was taught to use it. Since then, Danielle and pens have become inseparable friends. She is also partial to a good notebook.

Danielle is also (and always has been) an avid reader. This started with the likes of Jacqueline Wilson, Roald Dahl and Beatrix Potter, and expanded to include more authors than she could possibly remember. You will not find her without a book (or Kindle) in her hand, or somewhere in the near vicinity, and her bedroom is more of a library than a place to sleep. New books are an excellent way to bribe her. As is cake.

Danielle already works as a bookseller, but has ambitions to be both a published author, and to work in the publishing industry.

The Shade

It hadn't been a particularly peculiar day, up until then. I'd woken at 7.15, flung open the curtains, then eaten my unsweetened bran flakes, washed and dressed, going through the motions as usual. Not a hair was out of place.

Work was just that – work. Nothing out of the ordinary happened. I got in at 8.50 sharp, made phone calls, sent emails, collected post and tidied the office in the same way I do every day, of every week, of every year. Even the weather was perfectly ordinary – grey skies with a light drizzle – nothing unexpected for Perry Barr.

I'd gone through the day in my usual daydream state, not paying attention to much around me. I didn't need to – the routine was so engraved into me that I could easily go through the day with my eyes closed, and I wouldn't so much as trip over a shoelace. It was like muscle memory. So the last thing I expected was to end up tripping over my own shadow.

I left the office at 5.30 on the dot – nothing unusual yet – and made my way across to Perry Barr train station. Strangely, the train was already on the platform when I arrived – I was accustomed to at least a five-minute wait. I hurriedly paid for my ticket and made a dash for the doors, jumping on-board just before they slid shut.

Out of breath, I made my way to the nearest block of seats. The next thing I knew I was on the floor. Lifting my head, I looked behind me, but there was nothing there. Nothing I could possibly have tripped on, anyway.

Embarrassed, I picked myself up and brushed the dirt off my clothes, refusing to make eye contact with anyone in the carriage. I was all too aware that every eye was now on me, and I felt a hot blush creep up my cheeks.

'Busy day?' The woman opposite asked.

I jumped. I hadn't realised anyone was sitting where I'd intended to hide myself away.

'Not really.' I replied, still blushing fiercely.

'Thought not.'

The reply startled me, and I jerked my head up to confront her. The nerve of the woman! But when I caught sight of her, I choked on my retaliation. The woman I found myself faced with – was me.

I blinked several times. Hard. Squeezing my eyes shut so tightly they began to ache a little from the effort. When I opened them again, I was still there – sitting opposite myself.

It was almost like looking in the mirror – except for a couple of distinct differences. The Other Me had skin as pale as chalk, as though she'd never seen a ray in her life, and her hair was a shade darker than mine, which had been lightened by the rare fortnight of summer we'd experienced recently. But it was more than just that. Despite being next to the window, she looked as though she was trapped in her own little bubble of shade. Perry Barr was dull, but it wasn't that dull.

Staring at my doppelganger, I didn't know whether the urge to scream or to laugh manically was stronger. It's just so absurd, this woman couldn't possibly be my exact double.

Other Me coughed, clearing her throat, and I jumped so violently I fell off the end of the chair.

'Ah-hem,' she coughed again, which was pointless. She already had my attention. I glowered up at her from my patch of floor. Muttering, I picked myself up for the second time in as many minutes, and collapsed back onto the seat. But still I didn't take my eyes off the woman before me, like prey keeping tabs on its predator. I'm unashamed to admit I was afraid of her – I don't think that's an unreasonable reaction.

'Do you mind?' she said, finally breaking the silence. 'It's rather rude to stare.' She smirked, clearly enjoying herself. That snapped me out of it.

'So was your comment,' I shot back, the fear vanishing, only to be replaced by irritation, spreading like an itch. A sharp laugh erupted from her, and she covered her mouth, as though it had happened before she could stop it.

'No it wasn't. It was merely the truth,' she replied, matter-of-factly.

I bristled at that. Who the hell was this woman? 'You couldn't possibly know the truth of it. You don't even know me!'

'Don't I? Are you sure about that?' A sly smile crept across her face.

I opened my mouth to retaliate, but no words materialised. I was stumped. The truth of the matter was that no, I wasn't sure. Another mischievous giggle escaped from the Other Me, but this time she made no effort to suppress it.

'You're not, are you?'

'Not what?' I snapped.

'Ooh touchy!'

She actually winked at me when she said that.

'You're not sure that you don't know me,' she said, attempting to straighten her face, but failing.

'How could you possibly know me? I think I'd remember bumping into myself before now.'

'Oh, bumping into me before now would've been quite impossible, I'm afraid,' she said, the giggling resurfacing.

Well I'm glad one of us was amused. 'What on Earth do you mean, impossible? How can it be impossible? You're right here.'

'It would've been impossible because, up until today, I was you.'

I blinked at her. Had I just heard that right? The lunatic look-a-like genuinely believed she was me. I got up to move to another carriage, sure that if I took any more of this, what remained of my marbles would surely escape.

'Wait! Don't you want to know why?'

I spun around, incensed. After speaking so cryptically, now she wanted to share.

'Oh please, do enlighten me.'

'Because I'm your shadow. Or I was until this morning.'

Apparently she didn't get sarcasm. Figures.

'You're my what?' I said.

'Your shadow,' she repeated.

'My shadow?'

'Yep.'

I cupped my face in my palms. The crazy thing was, now that she'd said it, it didn't seem so crazy.

'Okay, so you're my shadow.'

'Yes, I just said that. Twice, I believe,' she said, rolling her eyes.

'Okay, fine. So why did you leave?'

She regarded me with disbelief, as though the answer was so obvious, it was practically kicking me in the shins.

'Maybe because you're boring? You are, you know. Boring,' she said, emphasizing the 'B'.

'I'm not boring,' I said, indignant.

'You must be. I wouldn't have left otherwise, would I?'

I shook my head, mouth hanging open. I had no idea what to say to my own shadow.

'No, you haven't tried to speak to me before. Maybe you should've – things mightn't be so bad,' she said, a pout replacing the smirk.

I was about to respond, but stopped short. What? I was sure I hadn't wondered that aloud. A realisation swept over me, and I felt the colour drain from my cheeks. 'Did you just read my mind?' I asked, unsure I wanted to know the answer.

'No,' she said. I almost heaved a sigh of relief, but she cut me short. 'I read our mind.'

Instead of sighing, I choked on the excess air I'd been holding. Our mind. Right.

'Would you have wanted me to speak to you?' I asked, over-looking the weird mind-reading trick for now. I wasn't sure I was ready to deal with that just yet – not on top of everything else I had yet to process. 'I don't think it's normal for people to have conversations with their shadow, do you?'

'Who knows? Not many people ever try,' she replied with a shrug. 'So you don't give it a chance to become normal.'

Something, other than the obvious, bothered me about what she'd just said, and it took a moment for me to work out what it was.

'Wait,' I said, 'not many people? Are you saying some people do?'

'Of course some people do!' She had that exasperated look on her face again. I shrunk back a little, ashamed of my apparent naivety, though I had no reason to be.

'You remember Bert?' She asked.

'The *Big Issue* seller?'

'Yep, that's the guy! He talks to his shadow all the time. Lucky Shade!'

Again she'd rendered me speechless.

'Wait a minute. Shade?'

'Yes, Shade,' she said, speaking slowly again, as though only just containing her frustration with me. 'That's what we call ourselves. "Shadow" just assumes that you're our masters, that you own us. But you don't, and we're out to prove it,' she said in a tone that implied she wouldn't hear any arguments on the matter. I was sorry I'd bought it up.

'Oh,' I said, unsure of what else to say. I paused for a moment. 'Well, if I treated you better – if we spoke more – would you come back? I'd feel a bit odd without a shadow.'

'Ha!' she barked. 'You're kidding, right? Nothing you could possibly offer would entice me back. Besides, I've promised Mary we'll go away together somewhere nice, finally get away from it all.'

'Mary? Who's Mary?' I asked.

'Don't you pay attention to anyone around you?' She shook her head, disappointed in me yet again. 'Mary is the receptionist at the front of your office block. Her Shade escaped last week. We've been planning our getaway for a while now. A week in Hawaii,' she grinned. 'We're at our strongest in sun as bright as that – it's glorious. Or so I imagine. You've never ventured out far enough for me to try it.'

I felt like she'd bitten me.

'Anyway, must dash,' she said, glancing at her glow-in-the-dark watch. 'This is my stop.'

We were at Birmingham New Street.

'There's Mary!' she yelled, waving frantically out the window at the shadowy figure I vaguely recognised, waiting on the platform. She gathered her black handbag – an exact copy of my own white one – stood, and moved towards the doors.

'Wait!' I yelled after her. 'You can't go!' I grabbed for her arm, but my hand went straight through it, and I stumbled, falling back onto the carriage floor. This was becoming an inconvenient habit.

This time I made no move to stand up again. I couldn't have anyway, even if I'd really wanted to. The shock of my hand moving, unobstructed, through her smoke-like skin had sapped me of my strength. So I just sat there, gaping up at her, my mouth opening and closing in its struggle to find words, but succeeding only in doing a damn good impression of a fish.

My shadow giggled, tucking a loose strand of hair behind her ear as she looked down at me. 'Don't wait up,' she said, winking. And then she was gone.

Danny McCann-Hale

Danny McCann-Hale is an English student interested in scriptwriting, poetry and the performing arts. He is influenced by writers ranging from Ted Hughes to Charles Bukowski, and modern performance poets such as Kate Tempest. He has written for London-based online magazines and runs a blog:
www.BlueBirdOnMySleeve.wordpress.com

Rhyme Ignore Reason

Do not force the issue,
now is not the time.

You've been coarsened by misuse
and reason's abandoned rhyme,

for its bedfellow, assonance.
And even though the sheets are yellowed,

his stifling, smothering arrogance
flickers doubt whilst blowing rhyme out.

Reject that man and his foolhardy ways:
scratch the match, ignite the light,
brazier the thatch and savour the fight;
Tomorrow is born today.

Reason must stay faithful to rhyme.
Still I have hope, but see no sign

Anonymous

Somewhere I Belong is an autobiographical extract submitted by a Birmingham City University BA English student who wishes to remain anonymous due to the subject and nature of her work.

Somewhere I Belong

The mind is in a **depressive** state and the **monster** inside rages to gain control. The 'Rock Chick' as my flatmate likes to call me, comes out at times like this. Piercings hidden underneath the hijab, and a tattoo – that's always covered – screams hope while the battle of the conscious begins.

'When this began I had nothing to say and I get lost in the nothingness inside me...' Mike Shinoda sings in the background of my living room up on the twelfth floor. I sit still. Well, as still as I can, with rock blaring in the background. My head is banging, vocal chords straining with all the screaming. And I say screaming because I cannot sing to save my life.

'... and the fault is my own and the fault is my own, I wanna heal I wanna feel like I'm close to something real, I wanna find something I wanted all along, somewhere I belong...'

The split personality in me is battling. Maybe Armageddon will come and everything will be okay?

* * *

The rational **voice** is attempting to be logical, and take over from the thousand other little demonic screeches that are nattering away in my mind:

'Stop being so damn depressing,' it says.

'You're luckier than most,' it says.

'You've lived through and survived worse,' it says.

'What do I have but negativity...'

So why does this feel so difficult then? I know shit happens and I know life goes on. But I'm sick of shit happening and I'm sick of just going on. **IT** takes its toll.

'… and the fault is my own…'

The **IT** is trauma; the fear and insecurities that are so well hidden, but which eat at me slowly. **They** claw with their long fingernails at the cages of my rib, trying to get at my heart and consume my soul. Sanity is at the edge. I lean over to look down below: see the damnation waiting. There is no way back. I'm losing my footing.

'… wanna let go of this pain I felt so long… somewhere I belong…' Linkin Park is a fitting soundtrack. I light a cigarette and begin to write.

* * *

Betrayal.

Such a strong word. I don't betray; I love fiercely and protectively. But that is the one thing I fear in others.

'I was confused… looking everywhere only to find that it's not the way I had imagined it all in my mind.'

I cannot stop this from happening. The **IT** transforming: losing control over memories, emotions.

A **voice** inside me says, 'Time to go.'

'No, no, please. No,' the **weaker voice** protests. **IT** loses.

'Just stuck hollow and alone… and the fault is my own.'

Time dissolves around me; the air particles break up and reappear in distant lands, in a distant time and place. In a distant moment I never want to revisit. The **Words** are a fading echo, reaching out to me in the darkness of the void: it sucks me in like a whirlwind. **They** condemn me. There is no consolation in the words anymore.

I look all around me. Who said teleportation wasn't possible? There is no astral projection, no higher realm of spirituality, no astral plane or outer-body experience. **IT** is the bitter **Truth** my life is based on.

I lie in a dark corner, caged inside the body of my **fourteen**

-year-old self, on the phone to my **mother** who is thousands of miles away in the comfortable surroundings of home. **HE** said that my mother had said it was okay for him to have sex with me. She wouldn't ever say that, I told him.

I can hear my own voice begging her. I beg to be **allowed** to come home.

'Put me in a corner of a room. Lock me up. I won't say a word. Just please let me come home. I'm sorry ami, I'm sorry.'

She doesn't reply. She doesn't console me. Instead she says go to school there. She doesn't say I can come home.

Home. I had no Home, as my step-dad would later remind me.

* * *

I go back further. I'm maybe three or four. There's a bottle in my mouth as I reach up to my uncle. He lived with us in our little home in Bradford. Mum was a single mother back then.

He tucks me into bed but something is wrong. Wrong below his waist.

It's around the same time: the milk bottle still in my mouth. Mum comes in. Did I pee myself? I don't know, but my tights, were they on or off? Was that blood trickling down my chubby little legs?

'I will never know myself until I do this on my own.'

* * *

I'm in the dark corner again, but Mum is not on the other end of the phone. **HE** is there in front of the door, not letting me out. His elder brother, my uncle, stands outside ignoring my cries, aiding him in his attempt to rape me. There are just the three of us in the house. I'm a million miles from home. From the normal English house I grew up in. I thought my uncle was a good man.

He was always nice to me – wasn't he? Or maybe he just played nice.

I scream. I cry. I hit out. I run. But where can I go? I try to hide in a big suitcase. He grabs me and pins me to the floor: strangles me.

'I started my period,' I protest. He wants to see my vagina. I'm losing consciousness, babbling about things I have lost all sense and knowledge of.

Their ultimate goal: to get their twenty-something paedophile brother to England one day.

* * *

I feel the cold laminate floor of my flat beneath me, and open my eyes.

I've made it back. But the music has stopped.

I go over to the mirror in my flatmate's room. I peel off my top and look at my back; seeking out the marks of the past.

'Don't think. Don't go back there,' the rational voice warns. Etched into my skin like invisible ink, the scars glow.

'Snap out of it! Am I back?' I think I am. This **voice** sounds like mine. I think.

* * *

I left home after my stepfather nearly killed me. He'd beaten me in the kitchen and come at me with a knife. My mother and sister saved me that night. My boyfriend called the police. I had brought shame on the family, you see. That was what having a boyfriend meant.

I couldn't take their shit anymore, the family and community's taunting eyes. Their questioning gazes, suspicious stares. **Their disgust**. Those who I had gone to school with, friends and extended family: always judging.

Hadn't I learnt my lesson the first time?

The young person's team and the police helped me move away as far as I could get. Life had taken me to a small town, full of white people. I miss it still, that small town where no one knew me. The beating that night was a blessing in disguise.

* * *

I hadn't spoken to my mother or family for six months. But I had to know, I *had* to know: had she allowed all of this to happen?

I ring my mother and cry and cry before I even say hello. She knows it's me. She cries too. We cry together. That's when I ask her.

She's **silent**, for just a second. **'What are you talking about? Why are you bringing the past up?'**

I'm silent. I stop crying. So she *had* known.

She chats on. She's happy to hear from me.

I say yeah, when she asks if I'm okay.

She says she misses me. They've been worried.

* * *

I put my top back on and make a cup of tea.

I want to think my mum had no choice. That it was the culture. Her life's been hard too. But a part of me died that day. A part of the family connection died too.

I still talk to them. Still do my daughterly duty. **People think I'm crazy**. I just say I'm Pakistani. I just say, it's **life**.

Sally Watson-Jones

Sally Watson-Jones spent some time as a child when younger, and found it fairly enjoyable, up to a point. Now an actual adult (in the eyes of the law anyway), she is hoping to do some writing and never have a proper job again. Sally writes non-fiction and plays.

How to be a Regular

A comprehensive guide to becoming a pub regular. Or, how to remain celibate forever.

If you've ever had the pleasure of working in a pub, you know you get to see more of the local wildlife than Chris Packham. There are many different categories of people that frequent pubs up and down the country, and whichever local you step into, you'll find similar characters. It's either reassuring or depressing that as people, we aren't all that different really. Especially when we've had a drink or five.

The best known type, is, of course, The Regular. Mostly men, although there are, of course, some women, and there are sure to be more in the future. If such a thing as a pub still exists in the future utopia, where nothing but party political broadcasts and lengthy enquiries into things that might not be quite right are funded by the public purse. We'll probably all be too skint to spend our evenings leaning against a bar and trading insults with people whose last names we don't know, or care about. But while there are still pubs, there'll be regulars, and regulars everywhere are pretty much the same. They've joined a club on the quiet. Unofficially, of course, but they're like all other clubs. There's an initiation, dues to be paid and rules you have to abide by. And if you don't, they'll kick you out.

For bar staff, regulars can be very helpful, believe it or not. They are always at the bar, so they see everything. They're there to stick up for you when some dickhead claims to have given you a twenty when they plainly only gave you a tenner. 'No you didn't mate,' from the bloke on the bar stool usually works to shut them up. Unless, of course, it's the regulars themselves claiming you've given them the wrong change. In that case, it's better just to agree and give them the change they think they're owed. They might be right and, even if they're not, the money that they've put into the till over the years is enough to make up for being the odd tenner down. Besides, regulars can expect a few pints on the house every now and then, if the landlord knows what he's doing.

It's not just argumentative customers that regulars can be helpful with. Intoxication can turn even lovely people into arseholes. And it turns arseholes into violent wankers. I've had lit cigarettes flicked at me when I've been behind the bar, threats of violence, people chucking glasses around, 14-year-olds demanding to be served, angry drunks insisting they have not had 'too mush'. Good regulars mean that even before the doorman turns up, you are pretty safe to laugh in the face of all this. You're the one serving the regulars their drinks, after all, and you're no good to them unconscious. If you're a bloke, they'll back you up, and if you're a girl, well, you can just grab yourself a coke and a packet of crisps and enjoy watching five regulars (that's usually the minimum number present at any given hour of the day) get rid of the knob that was giving you grief. Of course, if it's a woman on the attack, you're screwed. They're not going to get involved in that shit, so it's best just to figure out where you're going to hide, and a way to explain to the landlord why the place has been trashed and there's a dirty protest in place of the Smirnoff Ice that was in the fridge.

Regulars are also good company on a boring mid-week evening shift. As bar staff, you're kind of an honorary regular, (if you're around long enough), so you get to enjoy the banter too. Hours spent topping up the cordials, washing the drip trays and making sure all the crisps are facing the same direction are relieved by the conversation of a few regulars at the bar. A good regular can carry on a conversation with anyone: the pretentious students making a bit of extra money while they study the classics, the weird kitchen life form covered in strange downy hair and a layer of grease, and even the career-minded landlord just waiting for the brewery to put them in charge of a pub with a carvery and a kiddies play area.

You might think that all you have to do to be a regular is turn up regularly. The clue's in the name, right? No. Not right. Wrong. There were plenty of people who turned up at the same time every week, or even night, right when you expected them. You'd be hovering near the Bass pump with a pint glass in your hand, and it was always annoying if someone else turned up first and asked for a pint of lager and a glass of rosé. But though they were predictable, they weren't regulars. They were just blokes who came in at the same time, had a few drinks, read their paper, then buggered off.

The real regulars were the ones who were in the pub every day when their shift ended. They'd often leave their stuff behind their bar when they popped out for a few hours to do some shopping or go home for tea. Some of them had things delivered to the pub because they spent more time there than at home.

To become a regular and enter into the strange and hallowed club that is the same but different in every pub, you must pass the initiation. But before you can, there are a few criteria you must fulfil. You have to have the same drink every time. You can't really mix it up until you're an established regular and it's Christmas and you fancy a brandy. And your drink has to be a pint. It can't be a half because, frankly, that's pathetic. It definitely can't be a spirit and a mixer. This is mainly practical; not many people can down thirteen doubles without needing paramedic intervention - unless they're in a hard rock band from the 70s. Also, the pub must already be your local. You should know the place; you can't begin the initiation process if you don't know where the bogs are.

Once these criteria have been established, you can move on to the initiation itself, which consists of three basic steps. First, you go into your local, you order your 'usual' and if the bar staff know what that is, well done, you can tick that off and move on to the next stage. This is more difficult than it sounds as a lot of it rests on the bar staff you get. If they're new, forgetful or just bloody minded, you're screwed. You can't progress on to step two until you've got your usual without having to name it. Think of your beer as Voldemort.

The next step on the road to becoming a regular is to adopt and encourage a nickname. If you are trying to become a regular in an English pub and you have any Welsh, Irish or Scottish ancestry this is fairly easy, as long as you don't mind a vaguely racist nickname like Taff, Paddy or Jock. If this isn't for you then a physical characteristic is another good place to start. A huge moustache (this requires a fairly big commitment), thick glasses, a limp, being very tall (your nickname will be short arse), being very short (lanky), no hair, really long hair, badly dyed hair, or a strange penchant for wearing a tie with everything, even jogging bottoms and a denim jacket, all offer potential nicknames. If none of these apply (if they do, you don't have to admit it to me, just to yourself), then it is acceptable for your nickname to be a shortened version of your real name, Bri instead of Brian, Kev instead of Kevin, that sort of thing. By all means attempt a cool nickname, but trying to get a load of drunk blokes to call you Tex, Ace, The Mighty One, Big Dick or Colonel Amazing is more likely to end up with you being known as 'that twat no-one speaks to'.

Nickname established, you are finally ready for the last step.

Befriend a regular. You should become chums with at least one of the card-carrying members of the regulars club (there aren't really cards), but ideally as many as possible. If you can, go for the Alpha regular. They usually have a prime position, one of the only stools at the bar or the most comfortable chair nearest the radiator, and will often be the ones starting the banter. Banter is an integral part of being a regular. If you are fat and don't like being called fatso, lard arse, chunky, a drain on the National Health Service, or being asked how many kids you've eaten lately, then you might want to consider whether this is a club you really want to join. The same goes for baldness, shortness, tallness, wearing glasses, having any kind of disability, having a fat and/or ugly wife, being rubbish at drinking, having no job, having a shit job, and basically anything else really. In fact, banter may be the only point of being a regular. So, once you have been accepted by one of the regulars, they may buy you a drink. All you need to do is continue this all evening and then be the one to buy the last pint of the night. This may mean drinking more than you usually would, but it will be worth it. The objective is to leave with them owing you a drink, even if it means you take two sips of the pint they've just bought you, then quickly order two more just before the bar staff ring the bell and starts unscrewing the beer nozzles. That way, next time you're in, they already owe you one. And you're in. You're a regular. Cheers, you loser.

Natalie Sparrow

Natalie Sparrow is a first-year mature student on the BA English course at Birmingham City University. She is a busy mother and part-time barmaid/waitress. Any spare time that she has is devoted to Sci-Fi/Fantasy creative writing.

The Boy Who Changed Time

When I was a kid I remember my friend and me playing in the field that was over the way from my home. We would chase each other playing tag or just simply scare each other by hiding in the tall blades of grass. This one particular day we were playing hide and seek. We ran so far out of sight of my home that there was nothing but burnt yellow all around. The sun was low in the sky so we knew it was getting late but all we wanted to do was play. It was my turn to count so my friend went to hide; I counted to one hundred and shouted, 'Coming ready or not.'

I started running in all directions without looking where I was going, until I tripped over a tree stump that sent me falling to the ground. I looked up and realised I had run straight towards my friend who was stood paralysed looking at a magnificent manor that was directly in front of us. I had never come across this dwelling before and neither had my friend, but it was definitely there now and it was breathtakingly beautiful. It had a spectacular stone staircase leading up to a grand front door. The windows were alight with fire or so it seemed from way down here. It was around this point that I noticed it was dark and we needed to get home. So my friend and I regretfully left, hoping to find this place again and explore it further.

The next day we went over to the field looking for the house again. We searched and searched all day but could not find it. The games from the day before were forgotten; this was "hide and seek" on a much bigger scale. It was as though someone had removed the entire structure, foundations and all, and hidden them from me, never to be found. I did not even know why it was so important for me to find this house; all I knew was that my curiosity depended on it. Then, just as the sun was setting, there it was, silhouetted against the descending twilight sky. I walked towards the building to get a closer look and I gasped out loud at what I saw. Where stood a magnificent manor yesterday, were nothing but stones and ruins. It was incredible. I walked up the stone staircase that led to the front entrance and over the threshold. I gazed in wonder at the skeleton that was a shadow of its former glory. What had happened to this house in the twenty-four hours since I was here last? I blamed the change on my imagination, told myself that this was the way the house had been yesterday. However, my memory was strong and I remembered a light like fire that resembled life glowing within the windows, the staircase that looked like the opening of a heart, welcoming all that entered. I walked through each room taking in all that I saw, touching each carving on the wall, each crevice cratering the stone floor. It was beautiful.

I looked up and noticed pitch black darkness through the broken ceiling. It was time to go, I called my friend but he was no longer with me. I wondered when he had left, and then I tried to remember if he had been with me in the first place. I went into every room calling his name, but he was nowhere to be found. I began to panic. I ran outside, shouting his name, I turned around and saw the large dark shell looming over me, looking more malevolent and wicked than welcoming and beautiful. It was then that the night exploded into excitement. Noise over noise, sirens, and flashing lights and people... so many people. I was lying down and I could see the devastated manor in the distance, it was aflame: destructive, as bright and as deadly as the surface of the sun. I tried to sit up but someone was pushing me down. I looked to my side and there was a sheet. I did not want to see what was under that sheet, so I closed my eyes and drifted...

What was happening? That could not be my friend lying under the sheet! I was thinking hard trying to remember something.

What was it? I was here in my own memory while conscious. I sat up looking around me, trying to distinguish between what was real and what was not. It was starting to come back to me. The memories of revisiting this day hundreds of times before. I can remember an arsonist... an arsonist I knew I was here to find. I looked back at the sheet that my friend was concealed beneath and saw soot marks on the edges and felt the onset of rage welling up inside me. I had to focus. I stood up and as I did, realised that I was taller than my age should allow. Looking at my feet and hands I noticed that they were bigger than they should be. I paid no more attention to this and continued with my searching. This time I would not leave empty handed, the criminal would pay for his crimes. I made my way past the emergency workers towards the manor; I knew the flames would cause a great deal of pain but my body kept moving as if it were programmed into it like a computer. I could feel the burn at the edges of my soul before I even entered the building, the flames licking away trying to consume me. I had dealt with this before and knew how to handle it now. I closed my eyes and thought of the stream trickling slowly, cooling me as I walked over the threshold of the crumbling building, the stream that me and my friend had once played in.

I turned to the left and saw the fireplace which is where the fire had begun, the curtain pole still held in its fallen position leaning against the mantle with the heavy curtain material draped over the fireplace: the curtain being the main culprit in the fire's easy spreading. However, the fire-starter was still at large and needed to be punished for his mistake. I looked through the now curtain-less window and saw nothing but dark soot smearing the pane. This was too difficult. I was still too busy reliving the moment of near death, trembling at the loss of my friend. I closed my eyes and drowned out the rushing sound of the flames dancing around me, and spread out my senses.

I could hear something upstairs, a noise I had not heard before on my visits. It gave me hope. I ran upstairs. The room at the end of the long hallway was open. I walked down the corridor and as I reached the door I heard a muffled scream followed by a loud bang. I rushed into the room. There was my friend, hiding in the wardrobe that was falling apart. I screamed at him and grabbed his hand. Now I felt the searing hot flames double with intensity. I looked at the mirror on the inside of the wardrobe door; the reflection was gruesome, red hot blisters covered with black soot. I was burning. We were both burning. We had to get out. We ran to the window. It opened instantly and with ease. I was yelling and yelling. No one could see us, we were going to die. Smoke was clouding my eyes and then...

I woke up on the ground with a start; I looked around for my friend. He was next to me lying under a white sheet with soot marks on the edges. I knew who the arsonist was now; the arsonist was me. I looked down and shook my head. I put my head in my hands and rubbed my eyes. I looked at my hands; they were those of a child. I felt a tap on my shoulder and looked round. It was my friend, covered in soot. I had corrected my mistake. I smiled a small smile: I had saved him.

Jonathan Grupman

Jonathan Grupman is a second-year English and Creative Writing student at Birmingham City University. He has enjoyed writing from an early age, as he likes the idea of being able to write about whatever he wants without restraint, and also having the ability to create completely new worlds and characters, often inspired by people and events from his own life.

Plato's Cave

I stand here staring at the wall. Staring at the same shadows I have been staring at for the past twenty-eight years. Chains grasp my arms away from my chest, a brace holding my head, forcing my eyes towards that wall: those shadows on that wall. Dancing away in front of me, as if they are showing off their unobstructed freedom to my despair.

It's cold in here. Despite the fire behind me, it's cold. That fire. That fire showing me things on that wall I don't understand, and perhaps never will. All I have for company are the monotonous footsteps of the shadows behind me, and the faint memories of the times above ground.

Nicola Lindley

Nicola Lindley is an aspiring writer, teacher and baker. Things that take up her time, aside from studying and work, include baking, sleeping, obsessing over fictional characters, reading, writing and tending to her menagerie of pets.

Bake Me a Cake

Charlie thought of his craft as an art. Mixing ingredients, blending flavours, adding the finishing touches to the decorations. Baking was a very precise skill that he had a talent for. Baking was Charlie's hobby, his passion and his job. He worked at a little independent bakery and café, where he, with other likeminded people, served up all manner of baked goods for the steady stream of customers the café enjoyed.

Charlie was accomplished at his trade for a younger man. He could create cakes, breads, pies and all sorts of baked goods: they were works of art. He had a lot of experience and it ran in his family. It was his aunt that had decided to make a business out of baking and had opened Lettie's – a name meaning joy and happiness, and named after the owner herself. Charlie's aunt was a big, vibrant woman who, along with Charlie's mother, taught him everything he knew, encouraging him and ultimately leading him to pursue it as a job and livelihood.

Working at his aunt's bakery was the ideal job for Charlie. He was very much a people person. He knew all the regulars, knew their favourites and he loved his food being praised by them. Chatting up lots of girls as they came into the café on a daily basis was also a part of the job he enjoyed a lot.

It was getting near closing time one Friday. Charlie was cleaning the coffee machine and work surfaces when in walked a girl he was certain he had never seen before. He would have remembered her pretty little face and unusually bright orange hair.

Seeing it as his duty to entertain the girl, Charlie gave her his best smile as she approached him.

'Hello.'

'Hi,' she replied looking at the drinks board. 'Can I have a –'

'– Wait, don't tell me,' interrupted Charlie. 'Let me guess. I'm good at guessing people's favourite.'

'You guess people's favourite drink?'

'I can guess favourites. It's a special talent of mine. It's like a party trick.'

'Oh,' stammered the girl. 'Uh, okay… '

Leaning forward on the counter, he stared intently into her eyes. This wasn't entirely necessary, but Charlie liked to flirt. He kept up his gaze until she turned away. She tucked a few stray stands of hair behind her ear, blushing lightly. It didn't seem like she was used to that much attention.

'You're a latte girl, with a dash of hazelnut,' Charlie declared. 'Am I right?'

Her brows raised in surprise.

Charlie revelled in her look of astonishment.

'Very good!'

'Coming right up then, sweetheart.'

Her blush deepened, and she decided to focus on some of the other café's patrons.

'So, what's your name?' Charlie asked as he set about making the girl's latte.

'Noelle.'

'Unusual. I like it. It's pretty.'

'Thanks.'

'I'm Charlie, by the way.'

'I know. It's on your name badge.'

Charlie laughed. Latte finished, he bought it over to Noelle.

'Smart. No one looks at these things usually,' he said plucking at the label. 'My aunt likes them so we wear them.'

By now the café was practically empty. It was only the two of them and a few of the staff. Feeling confident, after guessing Noelle's favourite drink right, Charlie decided to have a go at guessing her favourite dessert. He brought out a large slice of Black Forest gateau. With its rich chocolate sponge and smooth cream filling combined with the sweetness of cherries, it had to be Noelle's favourite.

'Your favourite right? It's on me,' he told her with a wink.

Noelle looked back and forth between Charlie and the slab of cake in front of her with a smile.

'I do like Black Forest gateau, but it's not my favourite,' she told him with a laugh.

Charlie had never once got someone's favourite dessert wrong before. He was staggered that his talent had failed him. He casually told Noelle that he was having an off day and dismissed it, then made her promise to come back the next day when he could guess again.

Noelle left saying she would be back at the same time, still smiling to herself.

The challenge was on.

The next day Noelle returned as promised and ordered a spiced pumpkin latte. Charlie offered her a generous slice of Strawberry Torte, proclaiming it was her favourite dessert.

Noelle shook her head, laughing. 'Sorry, but wrong again.'

She accepted the torte though and gave her compliments to Charlie, who was feeling a little put out. He had been so certain that the sweet, creamy melt-in-your-mouth torte with its crumbly biscuit base was the perfect choice for a girl such as Noelle.

Noelle left a while after closing time that night, after having a very long conversation about food and baking with Charlie. She promised to be back again tomorrow for him to guess again, and Charlie took her crockery into the back to be washed where he found his aunt kneading some bread.

'See you've made a new friend,' Lettie said with a knowing smile, that disappeared when she saw his slightly sour mood,

'What's the matter?'

'Just a little annoyed at myself,' he replied, explaining to Lettie about getting Noelle's cake wrong.

Lettie thought for a minute. 'Do you think that maybe you're getting it wrong on purpose? So she'll keep coming back?'

Charlie thought about this a lot on the way back to his flat and when he got there he spent the rest of the night pouring over his collection of cake recipes. As it got late, Charlie came across his own favourite cake – vanilla, raspberry and blueberry cheese-cake. He lingered over it, allowing himself to remember the soft, smooth and creamy top with the added sweet sharpness of the raspberries and how the soft juicy taste of blueberries created absolute blissful harmony in the mouth, together with the crunchy biscuit base. He thought about baking it for Noelle tomorrow but decided against it. It was an unusual recipe after all, and the chances were that Noelle had never even tried it. He found himself wondering if Noelle would be able to bake something like this and if his favourite cake would be just as good if baked by her.

The next day, when Noelle came back, she ordered a mocha with a dash of amaretto. When Charlie didn't bring out any cake she was a little surprised.

'No cake for me then?' she asked playfully pouting.

'I always have cake for you,' Charlie replied. 'But this time, if I don't get it right, you have to bake something for me.'

Noelle leaned back in her chair, feigning aloofness but Charlie could see she was thinking about it.

'You're on. I suppose it's only fair. You have been giving me free cake.'

So Charlie brought out a slab of coffee cake, topped with thick coffee butter-cream and whole walnuts. The smell of sweetened coffee followed him through the shop, turning the heads of other customers as he walked by. This time Charlie knew he was probably wrong and why. But he didn't mind. He found he quite liked the idea of baking for Noelle.

Sliding into the seat opposite, he offered her the coffee cake. Noelle gave him that adorably sheepish grin he had become used to.

'I'm wrong again aren't I?'

She looked hesitant. 'I'm not trying to get out of our agreement or anything, but I don't think anything I bake will be as good as yours...'

Charlie handed her a dessert fork. 'Don't worry about that. I'm sure I'll like anything you bake,' he told her gently.

Noelle cocked an eyebrow in suspicion, then smiled back at him before dropping her gaze and blushing.

Charlie rushed into the back of the café and fished out the recipe for vanilla, raspberry and blueberry cheesecake. When he came back to Noelle he placed the well-worn paper in front of her.

'You're kidding,' said Noelle.

'What? Why?' Charlie asked, thinking the recipe might be too difficult for Noelle.

She burst into a fit of laughter. 'I don't believe it. This is my favourite cake. I've never made it myself but my mum used to make it for me all the time.'

'Well, now's your chance to learn how,' said Charlie, a little astonished.

Noelle frowned a little as she looked at the crumpled bit of paper. 'But... I really don't know how to make this.'

'Nothing for it then,' Charlie's voice was mockingly sombre. 'I suppose I'll have to teach you how to bake it.'

And he led Noelle off into the kitchen.

Verity Anne Cary

Verity Anne Cary is an undergraduate BA hons student of English and Drama. She has a keen interest in creative writing of all descriptions, her main passion being poetry that 'creates audible thought.' Verity currently resides in her heart's home, Malvern, with her little boy.

Literary World

When you're a bird
You are not a bird
You're a plane
Or an arrow
A dart
A dot
A 'v'
You soar
On the wind
Like the rivers
Flow out to the sea
An unfinished sentence
You're an unspoken word
When really – you're a bird

Ellie Nicklen

Ellie Nicklen is a first-year English and Creative Writing student at City North Campus in Perry Barr. She is currently enjoying her degree but cannot quite say for sure what job she wants to do in the future. She can be found dancing round your local supermarket or driving badly through Birmingham. Ellie may be referred to as an airhead but aren't all the best writers a little eccentric?

32 Miles

This is the last time I'm asking you this. One last time. I'm not going to scream. I won't plead. I won't beg.

I won't. I won't.

I'm raw and I'm hurt. I drink whiskey and wine at night. Sometimes I'll do anything not to feel you. Alone in this house, there is nothing but the ticking of your cold, harsh clock. Spending time. Spending me. My pain leaks all over the floor, thick and empty. My nails glide over the marble counter. The grooves in the wood remind me of you. I smooth my fingers into the soft, hard wood. I'm cold. Hot. Numb but so awake. I wander the empty house with the ghost of my shadow. I want to sleep now. I toss and turn, searching for warmth. I'm freezing cold. I heat up the bed with the hairdryer. I pile the pillows high. I yearn for sleep in my tower.

I try. I try.

The neon red light tells me it's 3am. I smoke a cigarette, slowly letting the smoke escape through my lips. I romance about you. To be home would be heaven. To be with you lights me up like a match that's just been struck. Sudden and hot. Bright – even happy. I'm getting hotter. Too hot. I long to be there. Memories and images tighten my chest. I'm searing hot. Panic quickens my breathing.

I burn. I burn.

32 miles becomes 100 miles. 32 miles is now beyond reach. I think of the distance we have to face. It scares me. Sometimes, I'll get up at night. Get in my car. I'll drive till I'm home. The headlights will illuminate our house. I'll cry and cry. I'm too scared to come in. I swivel the house key in my fingers. The cold

metal of the key burns through my tears. I call your phone but no answer. I leave a voicemail. I'm crumbling as I speak into the silence. You've disappeared. I know you're coming back someday.

I know. I know.

I am still trying to find you. Love me again. I love you still. My memory is full of sirens. I remember that look on your face, the night I was in the crash. The smile you'd always wear was absent. But you stayed strong for me. As I stumbled out of the wreck – you were still strong. Even after everything that happened. I don't know how you do it.

I don't know. I don't.

You're so strong. You're my castle. You keep me safe when I'm crumbling and clinging to life. You bring out this smile and it's amazing. So resilient. So beautiful. I've always admired you. I've never told you that though. You've never believed in yourself one bit. I suppose you've always been vulnerable. But you never show anyone that side. Not your son. Not your mother. But sometimes you show me. And I hold you till the feeling subsides. You're shivering still. But you're calmer. We listen to the big, old, cold, hard clock ticking. The quiet feels good. So let me please. Just ask you. Don't say no. Save me. Save you. Stop spending the seconds and minutes. Stop spending me. Please. I won't beg you.

I won't. I won't.

Christopher Tiller

Christopher Tiller started writing five years back and wonders why he didn't start earlier. He has written two novels and is currently working on a third, which he hopes to complete by 2014. He has had works published in several anthologies and is currently seeking an agent for his book, *Still Waters*.

James

In the hallway her sons waited in anxious silence to see their mother, wanting to be with her yet frightened by what they could hear. The boys sat on the landing listening to her anguished cries; the pleading for the pain to stop, the midwife's firm encouraging words.

James was sure his mother would die, not that he had any understanding of what death meant, the true meaning of loss. When Trudy died, the mottled brown cross collie they had for ten years, he learned she would never come back, that she was now in heaven, a place where all God's creations go. The notion of his mother being with Trudy, and not with him, was something that had crept into his thoughts since Trudy's death.

James listened to his mother's screams, her every laboured word, as the hours slowly moved by. Outside, the wind rattled loose windows, groaned under doors and crept across the wooden floor, sweeping over his small bare feet. James slid across the boards pushing himself against his elder brother who threw an arm about his shoulder, telling him, 'Mom'll be fine, it's just the baby coming, that's all.'

The words didn't ease James' fear, didn't stop him wanting to run into his mother's bedroom and shout, 'Stop making mommy scream.' Instead, he sank deeper into his brother's arms, placing his small hands over his ears.

Jane Delore settled the baby on her breast, quieting the newborn. The wind dropped to a low-pitched whistle and the world calmed and slowed. The midwife stood in the doorway, her shadow gliding over the two small boys huddled in the hall outside.

'You've a brother,' she said smiling. 'Come on then, expect you want to see. Just for a while now as your mammy will be needing her rest. It's been a busy night for them both.'

James pushed his back tighter to the wall as his brother Peter stood and rushed past the tall women in the doorway. James shook his head, hands still clasped firmly over his ears, watching the midwife's mouth move soundlessly. She took a few steps forward, stretching out an arm to lift him from his sitting position. He tightened every muscle as fat fingers circled his delicate skinny wrist, pulling him up from the cold floor. He relaxed his small body, allowed himself to go limp. His arm airborne, suspended above his head, trapped in the grip of the midwife's hand.

Released, he scuttled back against the wall, placing hands back over his ears as words fell from the moving mouth of the giant standing in front of him. The giant crouched down to his level. Red smeared over white cloth. A smile, a grin. James slammed his eyes shut and screamed to make her go away. To make his mother come.

James opened his eyes and wrapped his small arms around his knees. The hall was empty, bigger than he'd ever remembered. An icy draught blew across his back and the only noise was an occasional groan from the dying wind outside. He listened to the calm low voices coming from his mother's room and slowly picked himself up from the cold floor. Taking small careful steps, he made his way to the door before pushing it slightly open and silently peering through the gap. He saw Peter sat on the edge of his mother's bed stretching out slender fingers to touch his new brother.

Jane smiled at her eldest son, her head resting against the pillowed headboard. She took Peter's hand, giving it a gentle squeeze, and asked, 'Where's James?'

The midwife cut in before Peter could answer. 'He's being silly, he won't come in. I've tried. He'll come to you when he's good and ready mind. Right, my job's pretty much done here, and you'll be needing some help for a day or two. Just till you're up on your feet.'

'I'll be fine. Peter will help.'

She lay on the bed holding the tiny bundle of cloth close to her chest. Calling to James, she offered her hand. He stepped in and stood still, gripping the door handle until his fingers hurt. His eyes moved from his mother to Peter, then to the parcel of white towelling, before he turned to run out.

James awoke to a darkened room. Rain gently patted the window and a watery moon danced its light across the bedroom floor. His brother Peter slept next to him. Short bursts of warm sweet breath swept across James' face.

He sat up, cried for his mother, but the night stayed silent. The rain played with the window, and his brother slept on.

Through the blue half-light, he crossed the hall, pushed open his mother's bedroom door, and entered another silent room. The object that had made his sleeping mother cry out, lay next to her, wrapped in a shawl.

James picked up the white bundle, the delicate scent of washing soap and sour milk filling his senses. He quietly carried the sleeping child into the cold hallway, stopping at the top of the wooden stairs.

'You hurt my mommy,' he whispered, as small slender arms went limp.

Acknowledgments

The editors would like to say thank you:

To our fearless leader Gregory Leadbetter. Without him, this anthology would not exist.

To Helen Cross for providing a beautiful foreword. It was more than we could have wished for.

To Samantha Malkin for all her help. We couldn't have done it without her support.

To the lecturers that have given up their time to provide us with prose, poetry and advice.

To everyone that submitted work. Without all of their contributions, this anthology would not be what it is.

To our friends and family for putting up with us. The creation of this book has been a rollercoaster, and without them we would have fallen off the crazy train.

And finally, to you. By purchasing this book, you are supporting blossoming writers. Feel proud of yourself, reader.